ᐊᒪᖅᑯᑦ ᓄᓇᖓᑦ

The Country of Wolves

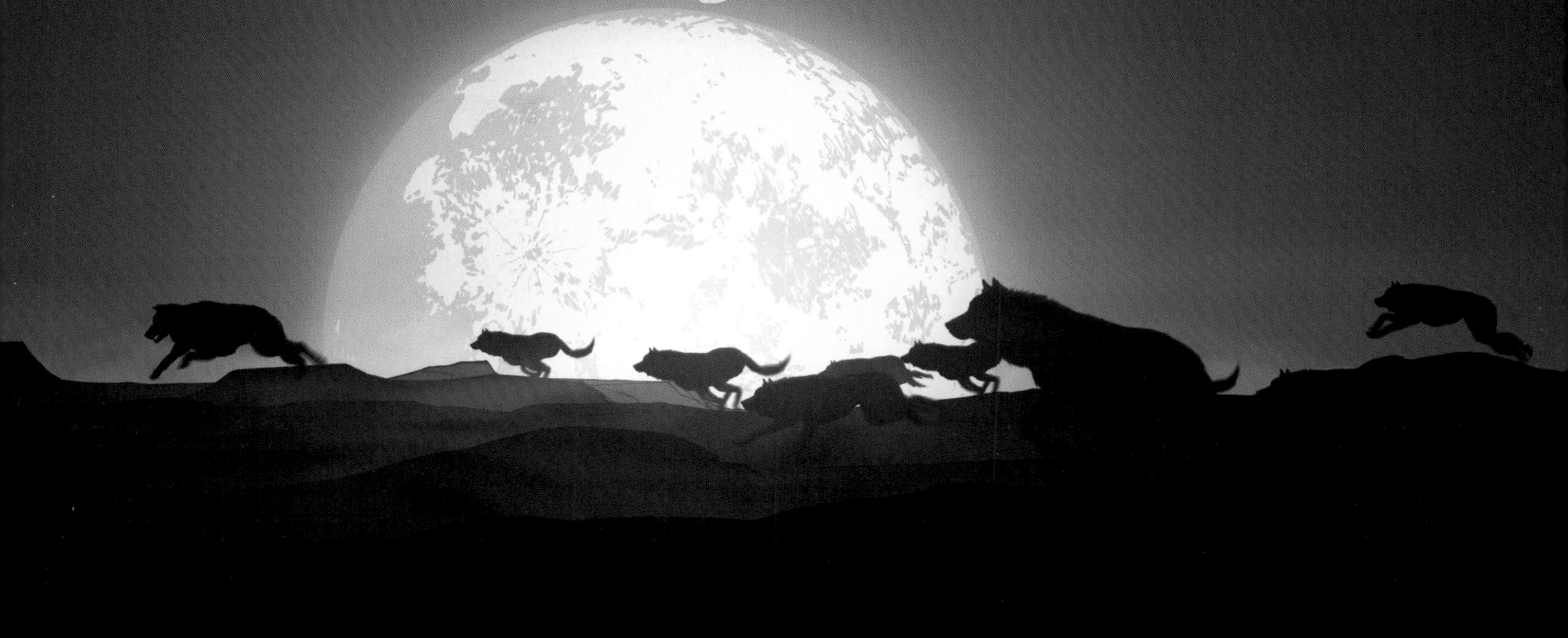

Published by Inhabit Media Inc.
www.inhabitmedia.com

Nunavut Office: P.O. Box 11125, Iqaluit, Nunavut, X0A 1H0
Ontario Office: 146A Orchard View Blvd., Toronto, Ontario, M4R 1C3

Editors: Louise Flaherty and Kelly Ward
Written by: Neil Christopher
Illustrations by: Ramón Pérez
Additional Work by: Daniel Gies

We acknowledge the support of the Canada Council for the Arts for our publishing program.

Printed in Canada.

Library and Archives Canada Cataloguing in Publication

Christopher, Neil, 1972-
The country of wolves / retold by Neil Christopher ; illustrated by Ramón Pérez ; additional work by Daniel Gies.

ISBN 978-1-927095-35-5

1. Graphic novels. I. Pérez, Ramón II. Title.

PN6733.C54C68 2013a j741.5'971 C2012-908466-2

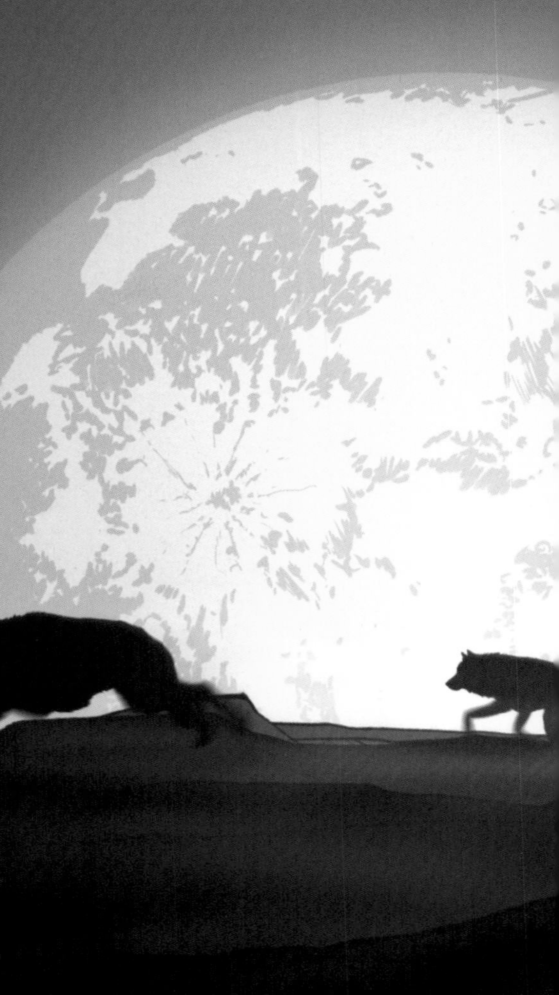

Canada

Canada Council Conseil des Arts

The Country of Wolves

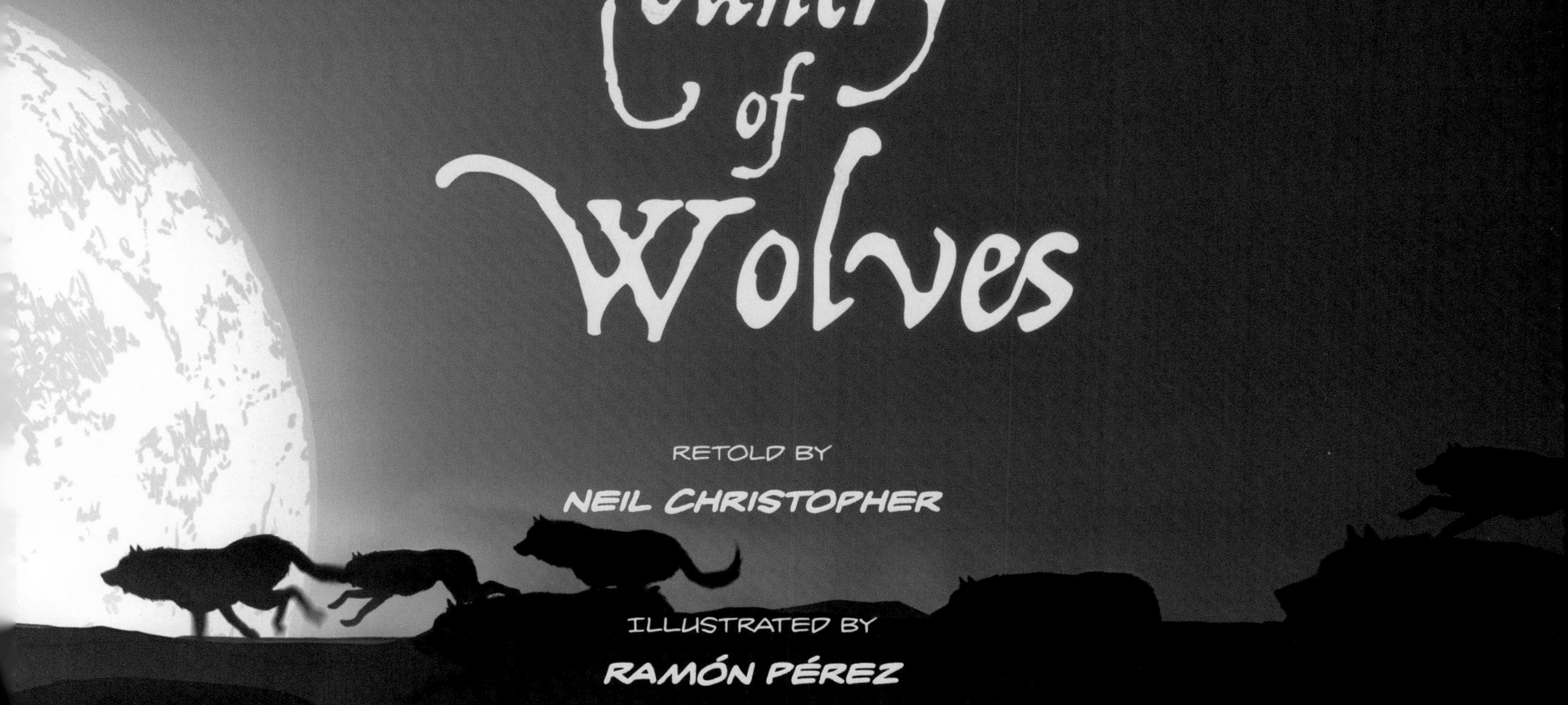

RETOLD BY

NEIL CHRISTOPHER

ILLUSTRATED BY

RAMÓN PÉREZ

ADDITIONAL WORK BY

DANIEL GIES

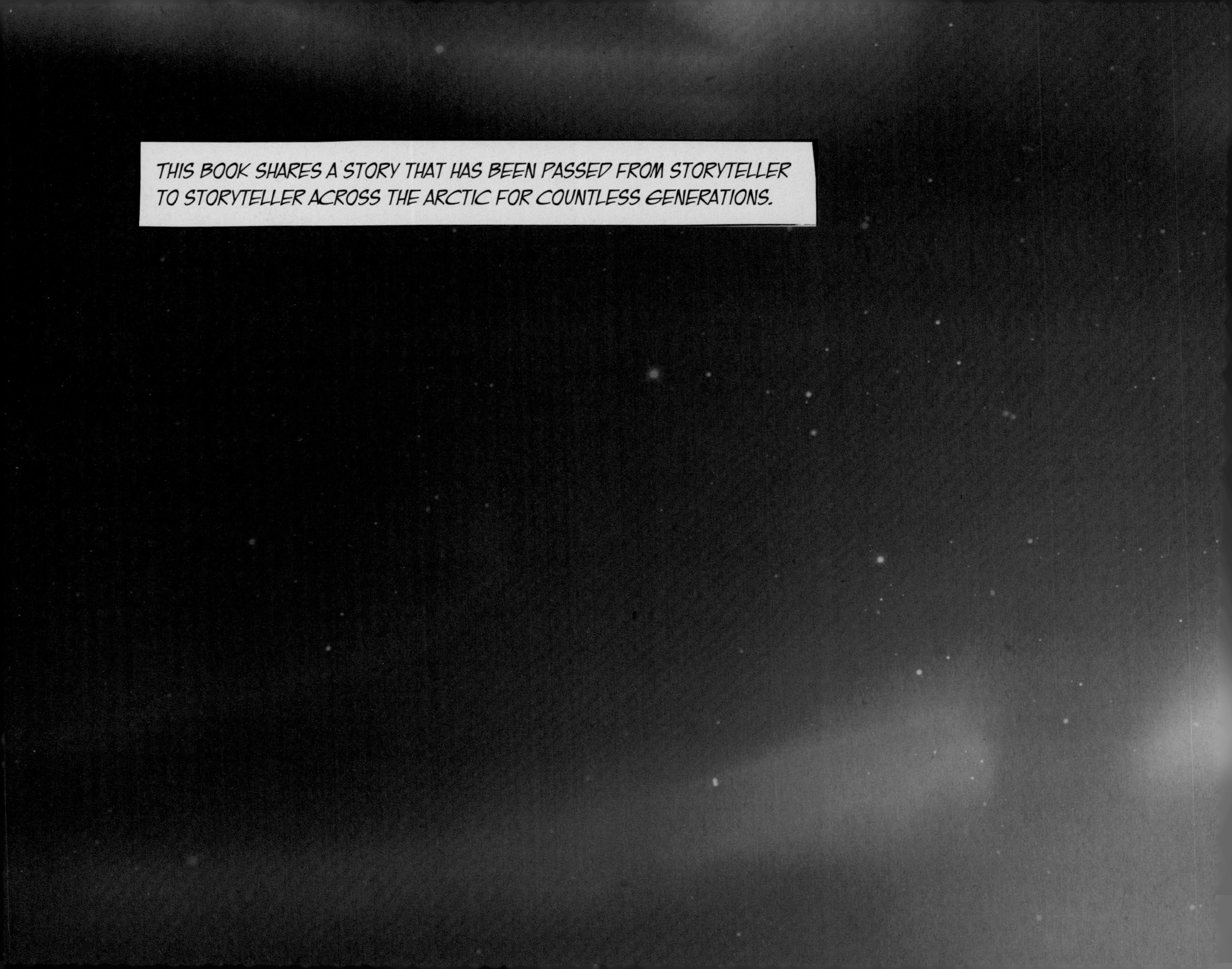
THIS BOOK SHARES A STORY THAT HAS BEEN PASSED FROM STORYTELLER TO STORYTELLER ACROSS THE ARCTIC FOR COUNTLESS GENERATIONS.

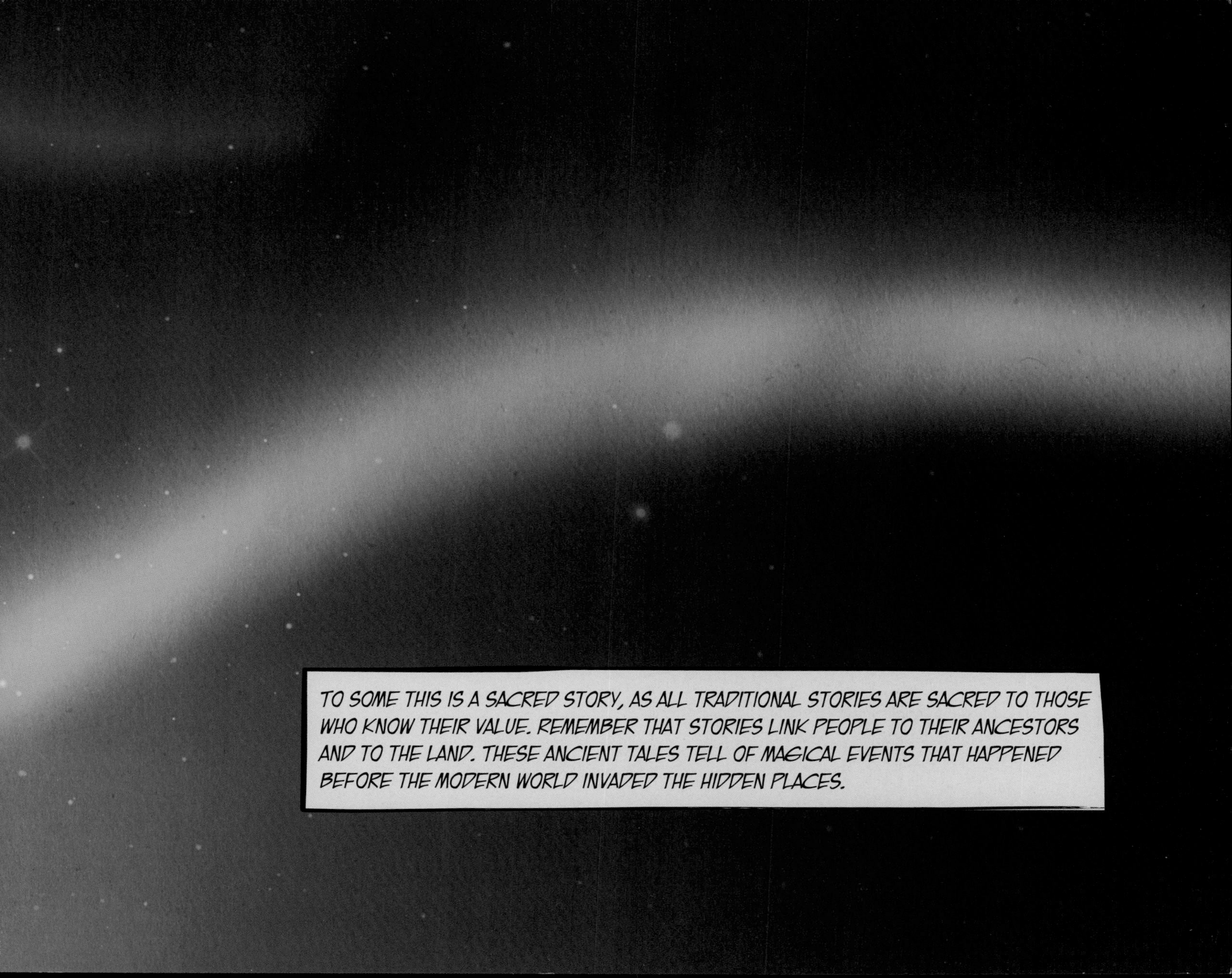
TO SOME THIS IS A SACRED STORY, AS ALL TRADITIONAL STORIES ARE SACRED TO THOSE WHO KNOW THEIR VALUE. REMEMBER THAT STORIES LINK PEOPLE TO THEIR ANCESTORS AND TO THE LAND. THESE ANCIENT TALES TELL OF MAGICAL EVENTS THAT HAPPENED BEFORE THE MODERN WORLD INVADED THE HIDDEN PLACES.

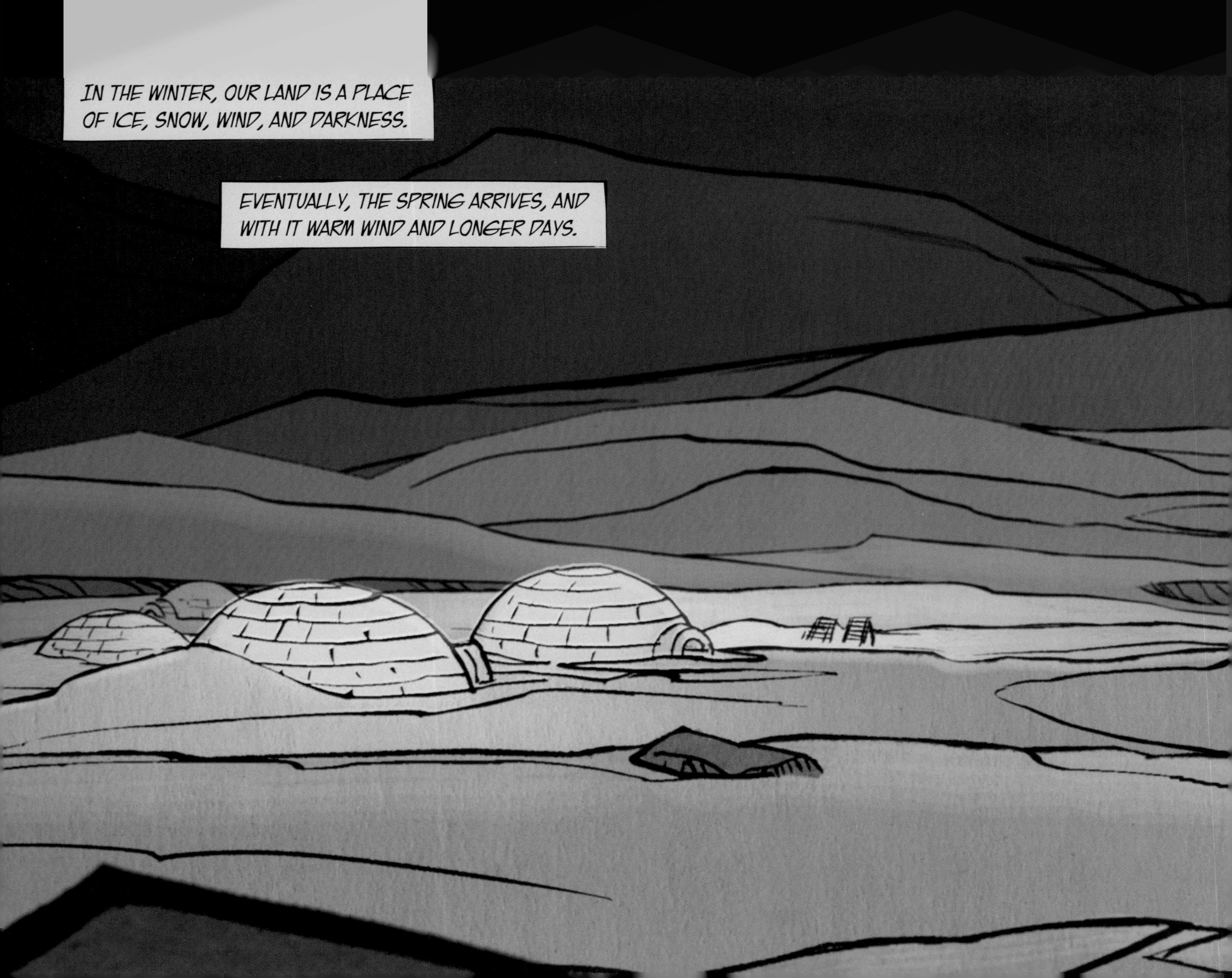
IN THE WINTER, OUR LAND IS A PLACE OF ICE, SNOW, WIND, AND DARKNESS.
EVENTUALLY, THE SPRING ARRIVES, AND WITH IT WARM WIND AND LONGER DAYS.

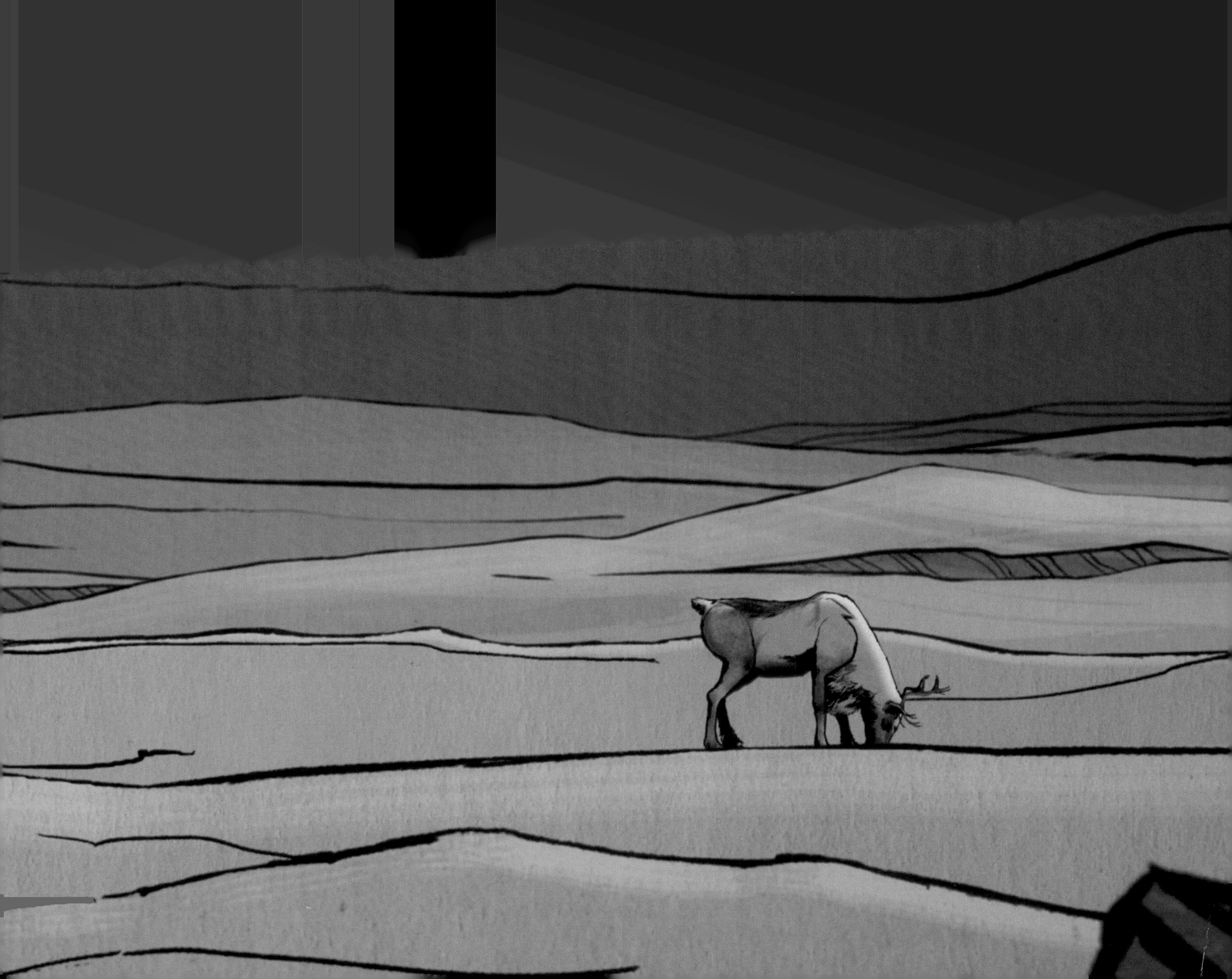

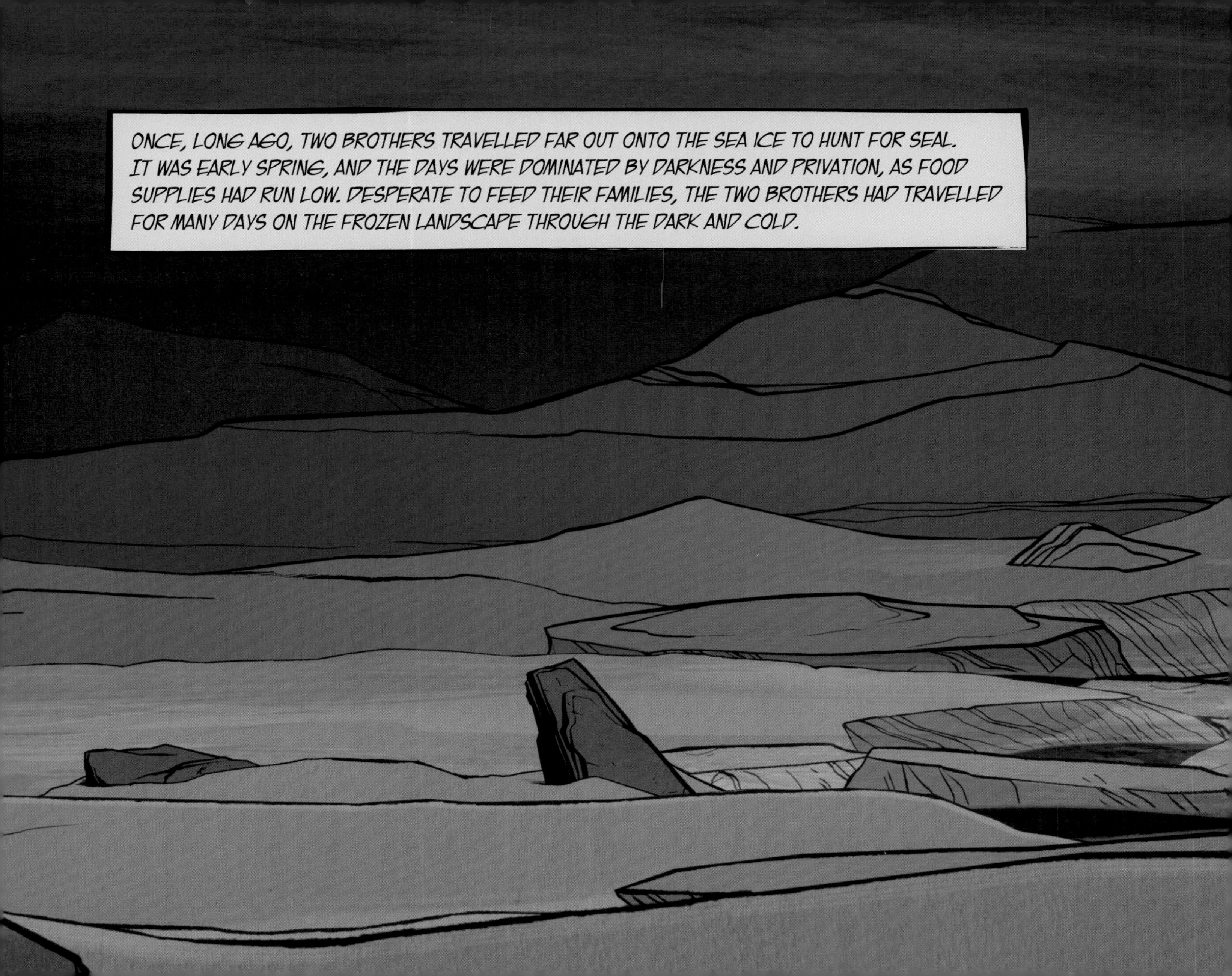
ONCE, LONG AGO, TWO BROTHERS TRAVELLED FAR OUT ONTO THE SEA ICE TO HUNT FOR SEAL. IT WAS EARLY SPRING, AND THE DAYS WERE DOMINATED BY DARKNESS AND PRIVATION, AS FOOD SUPPLIES HAD RUN LOW. DESPERATE TO FEED THEIR FAMILIES, THE TWO BROTHERS HAD TRAVELLED FOR MANY DAYS ON THE FROZEN LANDSCAPE THROUGH THE DARK AND COLD.

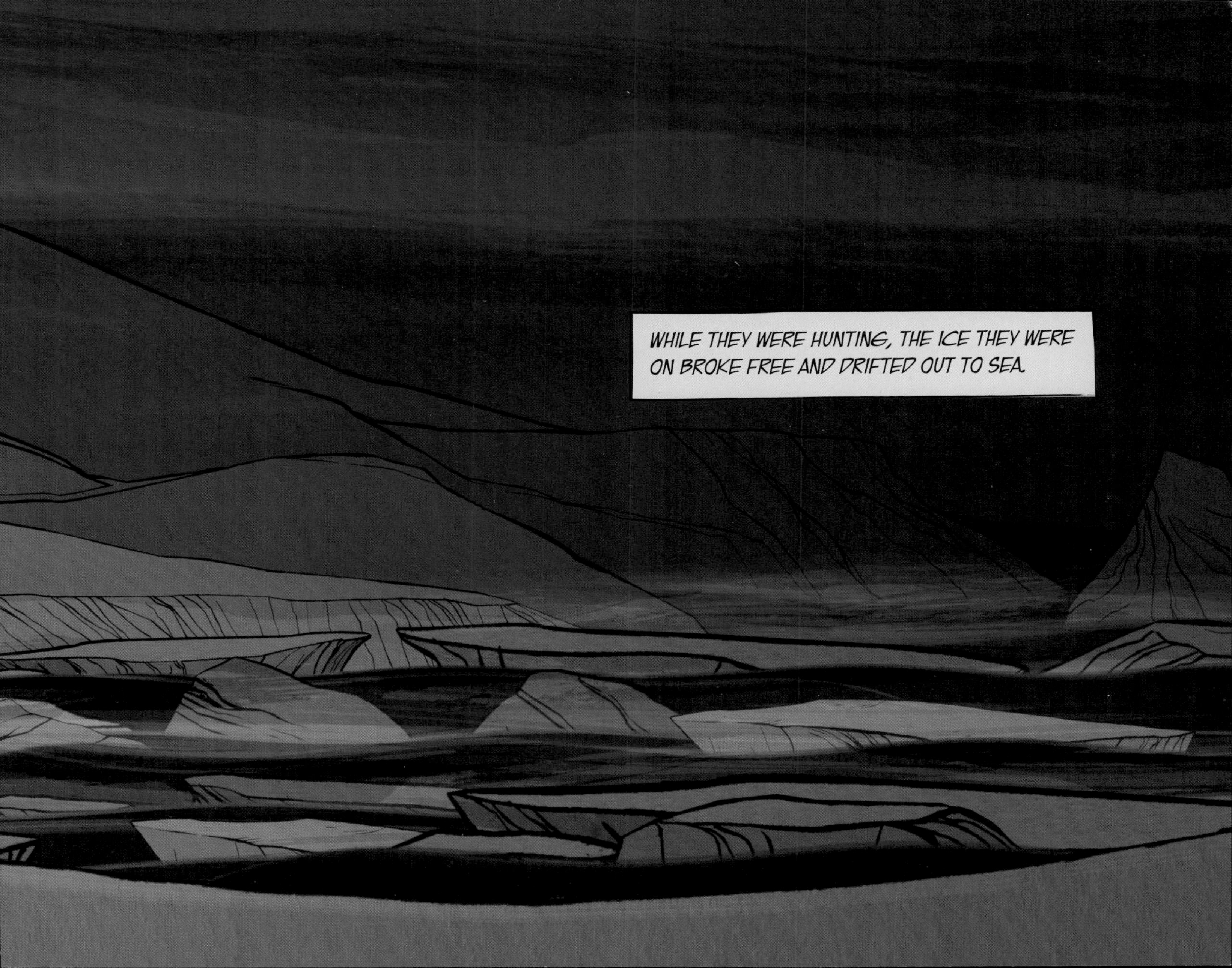
WHILE THEY WERE HUNTING, THE ICE THEY WERE ON BROKE FREE AND DRIFTED OUT TO SEA.

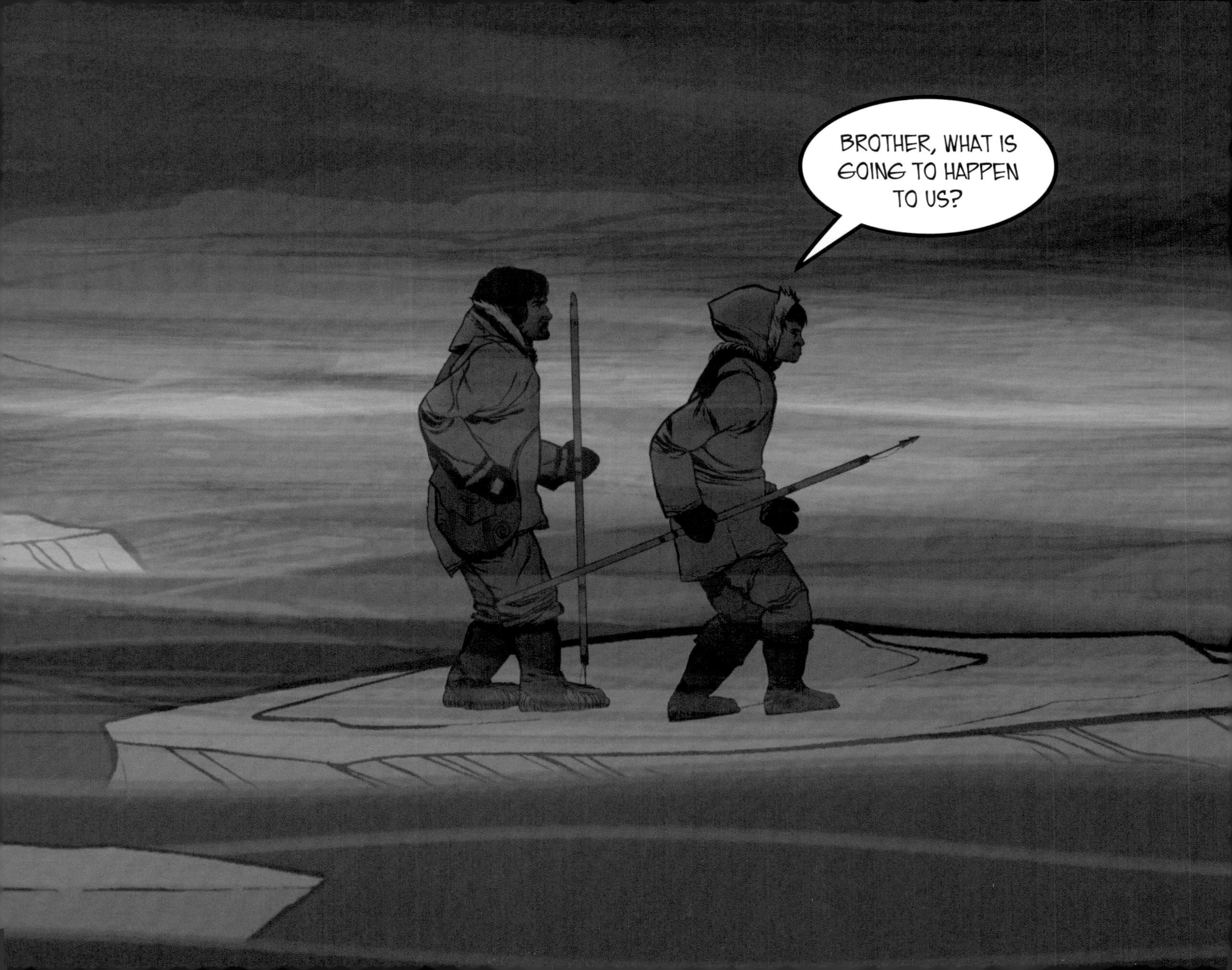
BROTHER, WHAT IS GOING TO HAPPEN TO US?

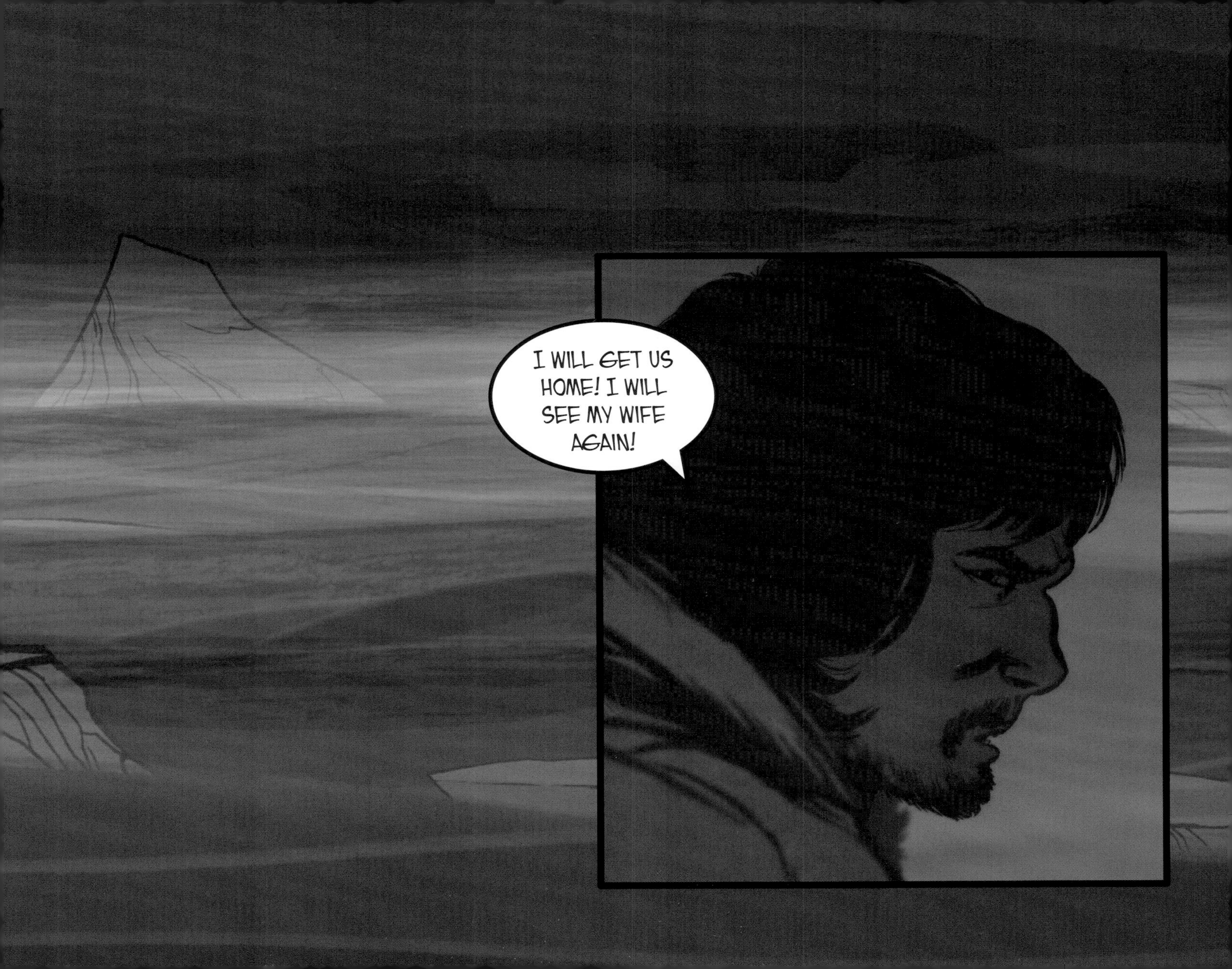
I WILL GET US HOME! I WILL SEE MY WIFE AGAIN!

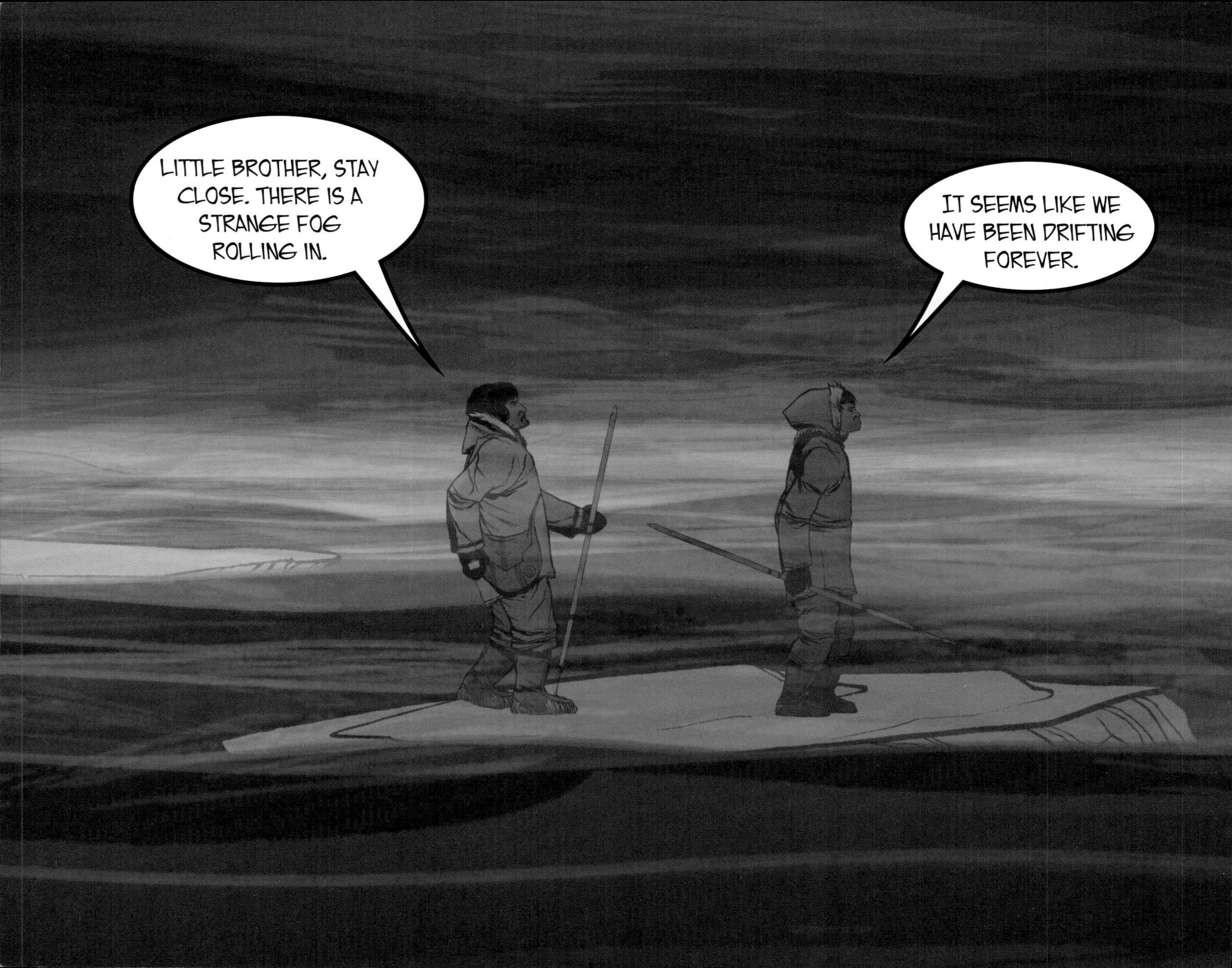
LITTLE BROTHER, STAY CLOSE. THERE IS A STRANGE FOG ROLLING IN.
IT SEEMS LIKE WE HAVE BEEN DRIFTING FOREVER.

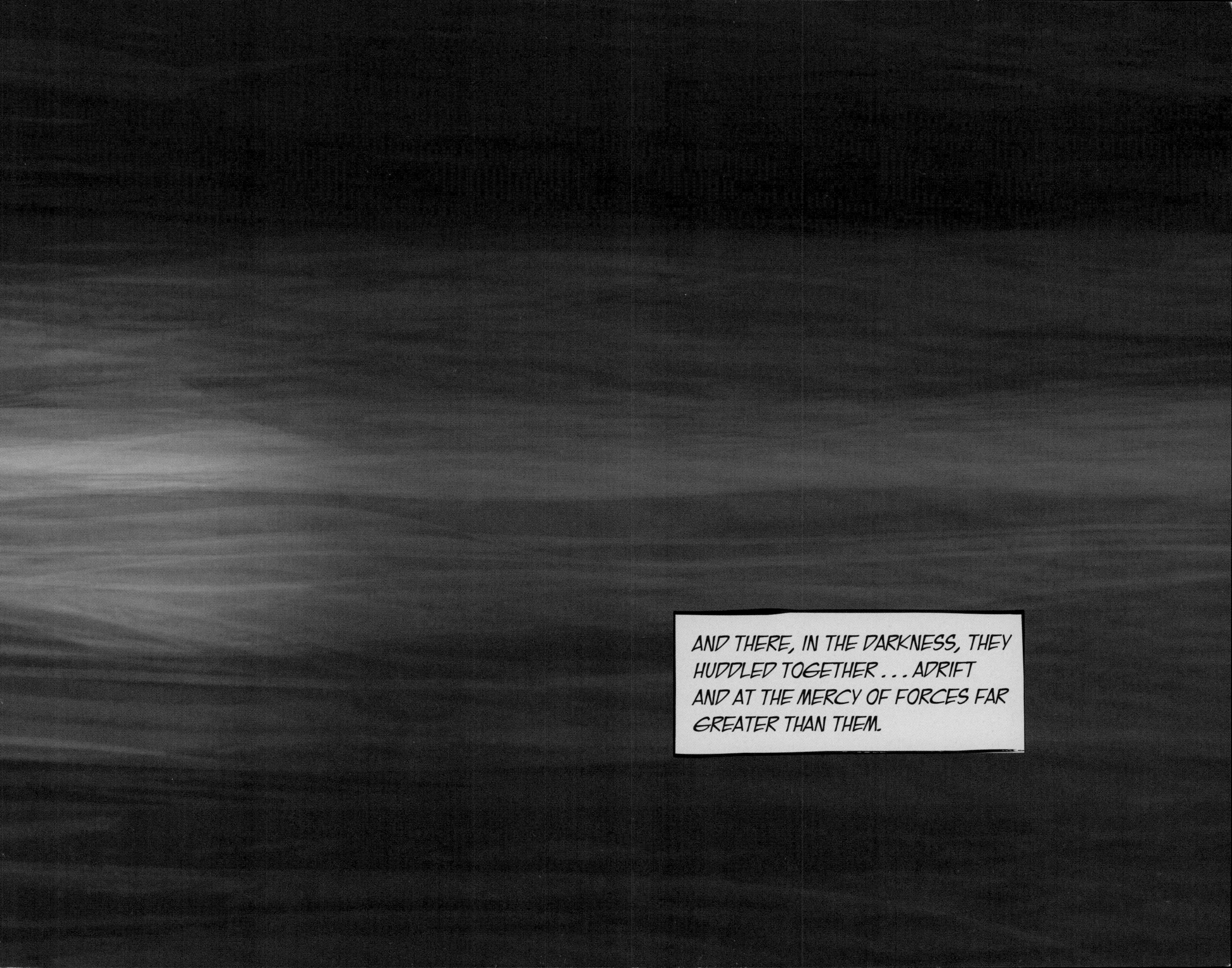
AND THERE, IN THE DARKNESS, THEY HUDDLED TOGETHER . . . ADRIFT AND AT THE MERCY OF FORCES FAR GREATER THAN THEM.

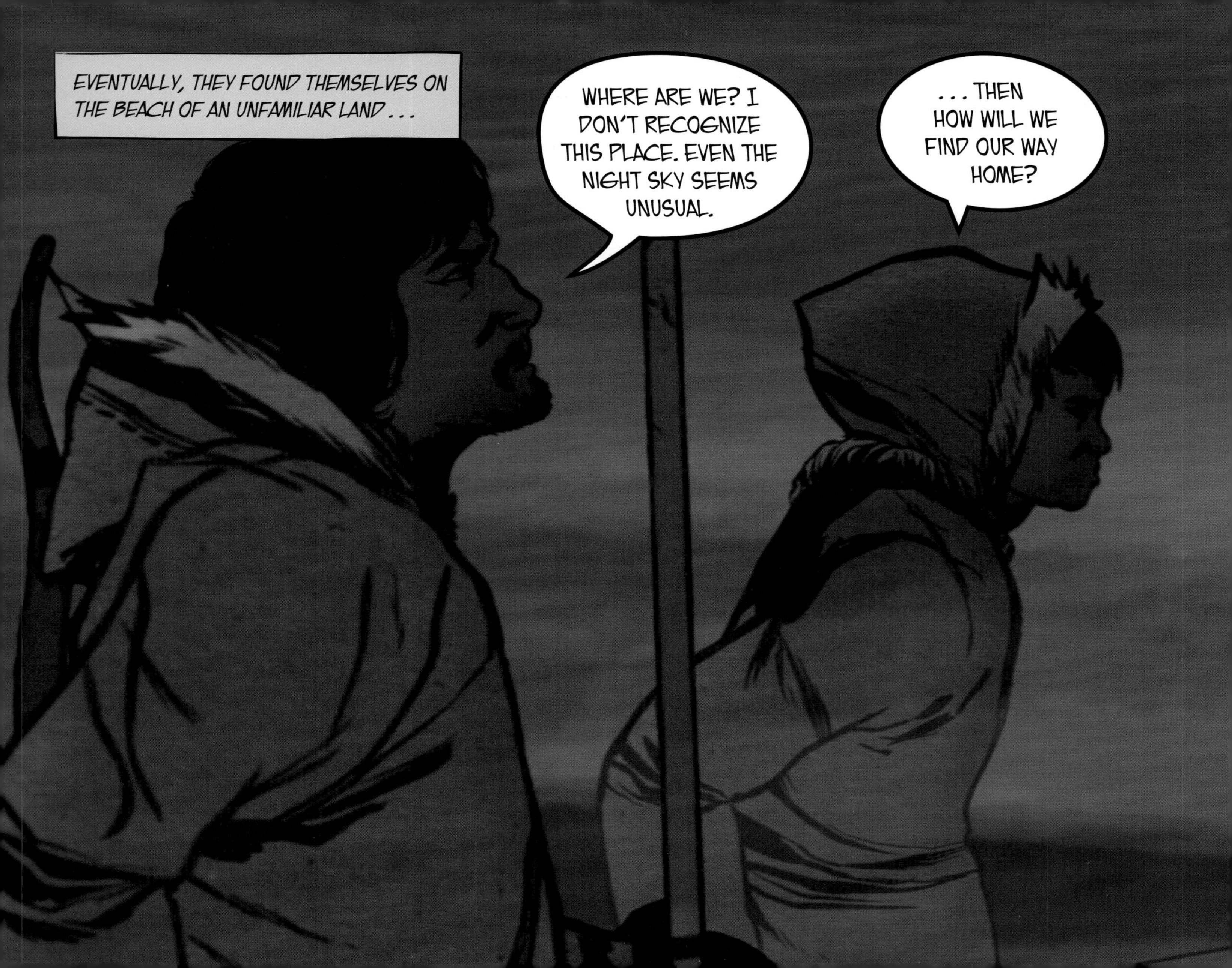
EVENTUALLY, THEY FOUND THEMSELVES ON THE BEACH OF AN UNFAMILIAR LAND . . .
WHERE ARE WE? I DON'T RECOGNIZE THIS PLACE. EVEN THE NIGHT SKY SEEMS UNUSUAL.
. . . THEN HOW WILL WE FIND OUR WAY HOME?

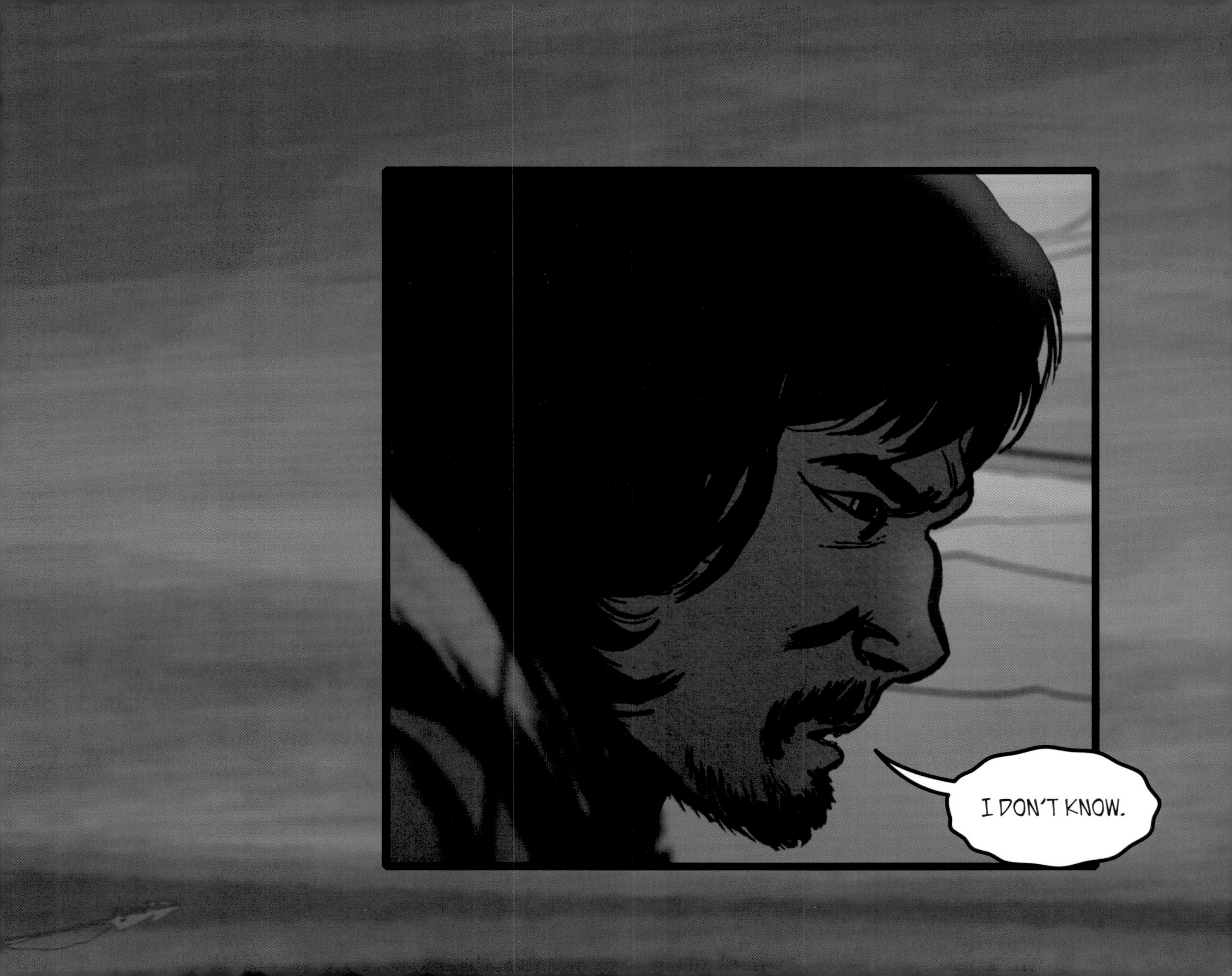
I DON'T KNOW.

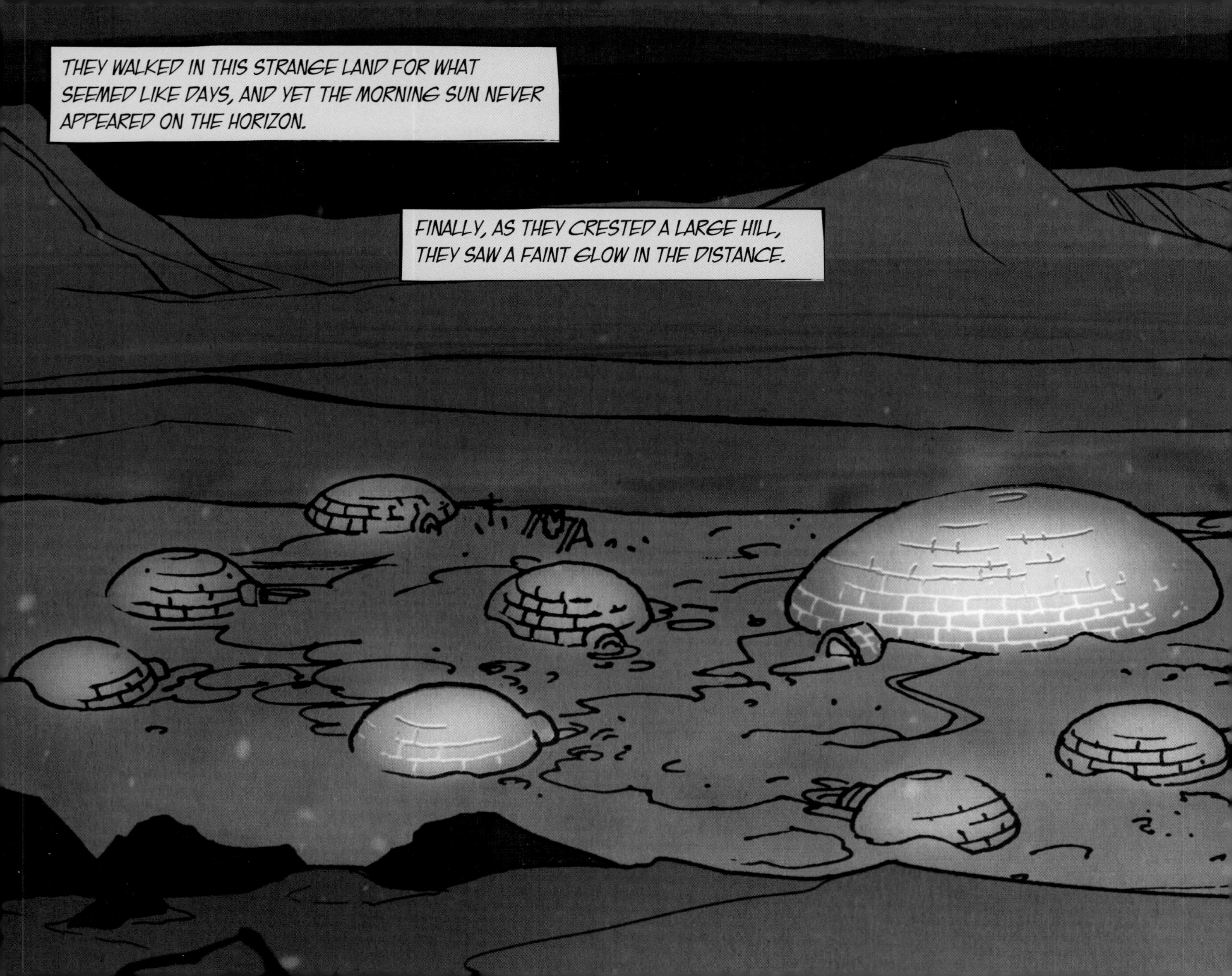
THEY WALKED IN THIS STRANGE LAND FOR WHAT SEEMED LIKE DAYS, AND YET THE MORNING SUN NEVER APPEARED ON THE HORIZON.
FINALLY, AS THEY CRESTED A LARGE HILL, THEY SAW A FAINT GLOW IN THE DISTANCE.

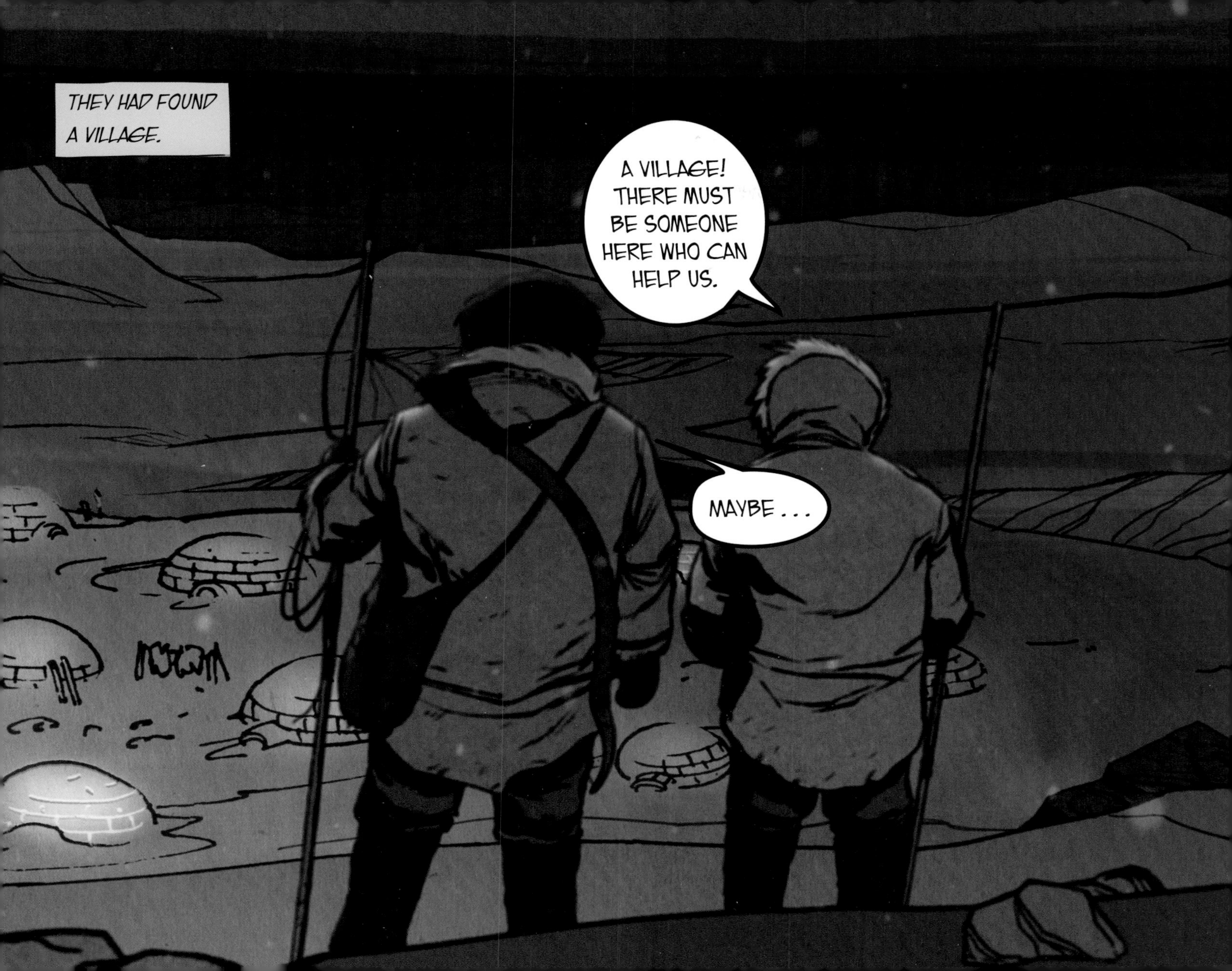
THEY HAD FOUND A VILLAGE.
A VILLAGE! THERE MUST BE SOMEONE HERE WHO CAN HELP US.
MAYBE . . .

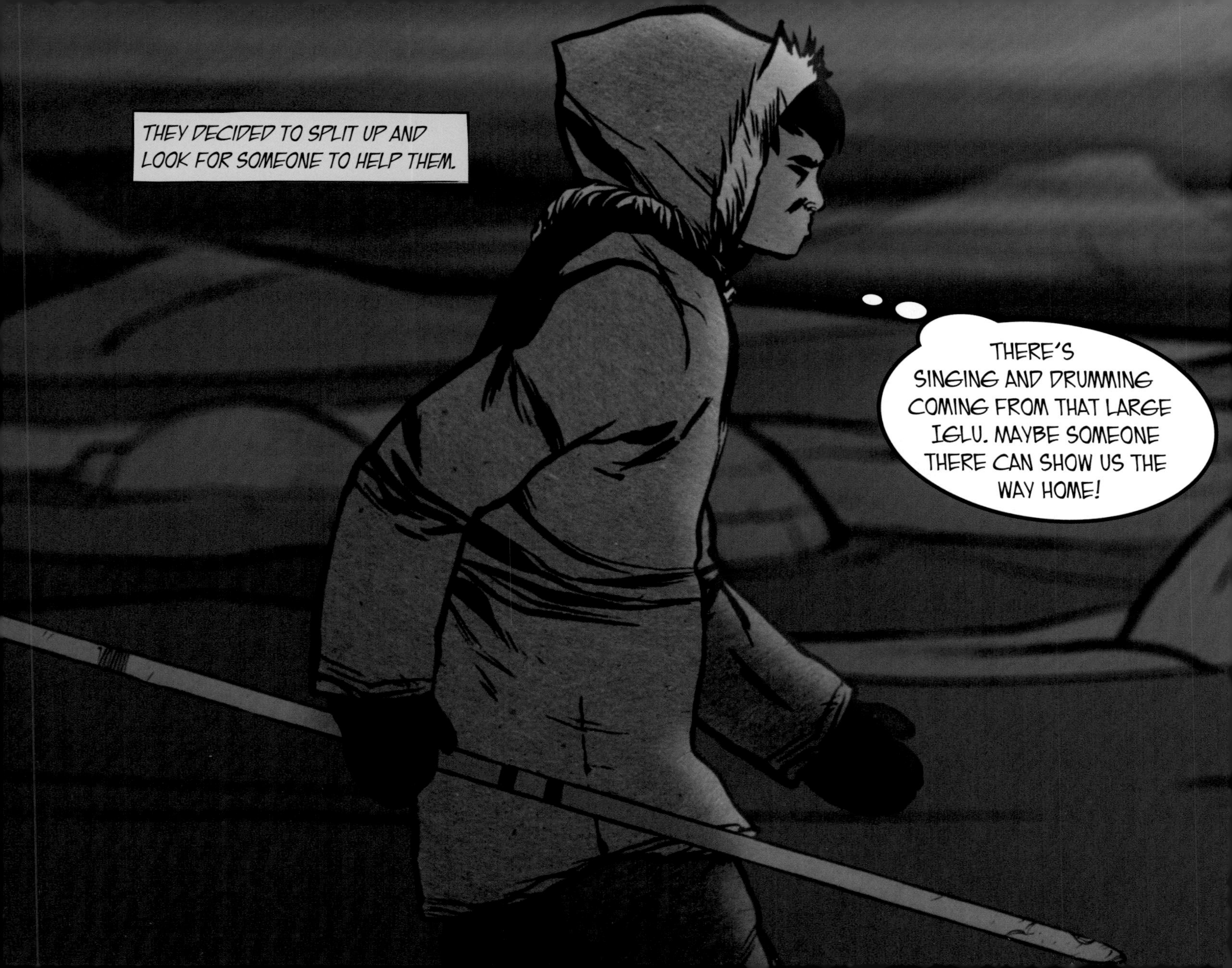
THEY DECIDED TO SPLIT UP AND LOOK FOR SOMEONE TO HELP THEM.
THERE'S SINGING AND DRUMMING COMING FROM THAT LARGE IGLU. MAYBE SOMEONE THERE CAN SHOW US THE WAY HOME!

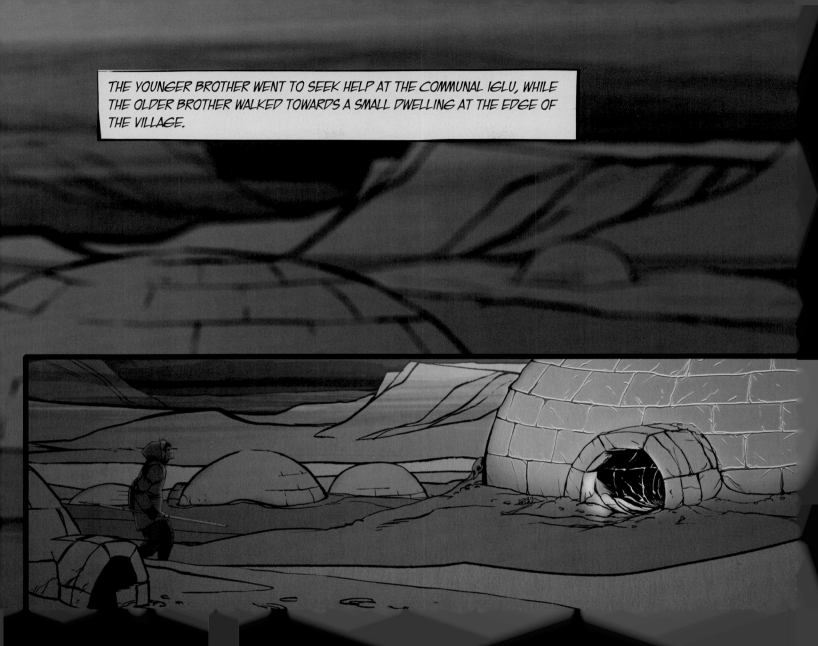

THE YOUNGER BROTHER WENT TO SEEK HELP AT THE COMMUNAL IGLU, WHILE THE OLDER BROTHER WALKED TOWARDS A SMALL DWELLING AT THE EDGE OF THE VILLAGE.

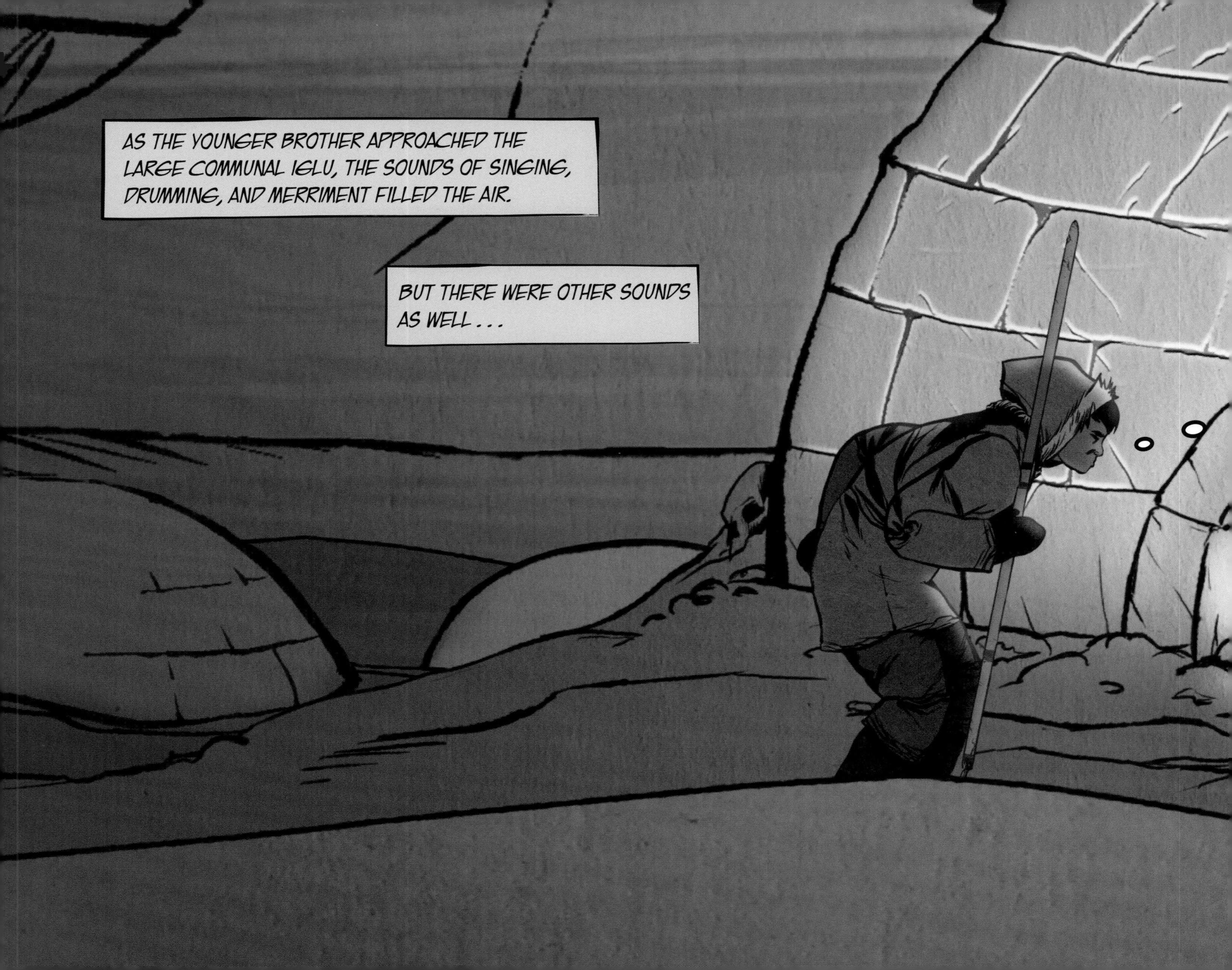
AS THE YOUNGER BROTHER APPROACHED THE LARGE COMMUNAL IGLU, THE SOUNDS OF SINGING, DRUMMING, AND MERRIMENT FILLED THE AIR.
BUT THERE WERE OTHER SOUNDS AS WELL . . .

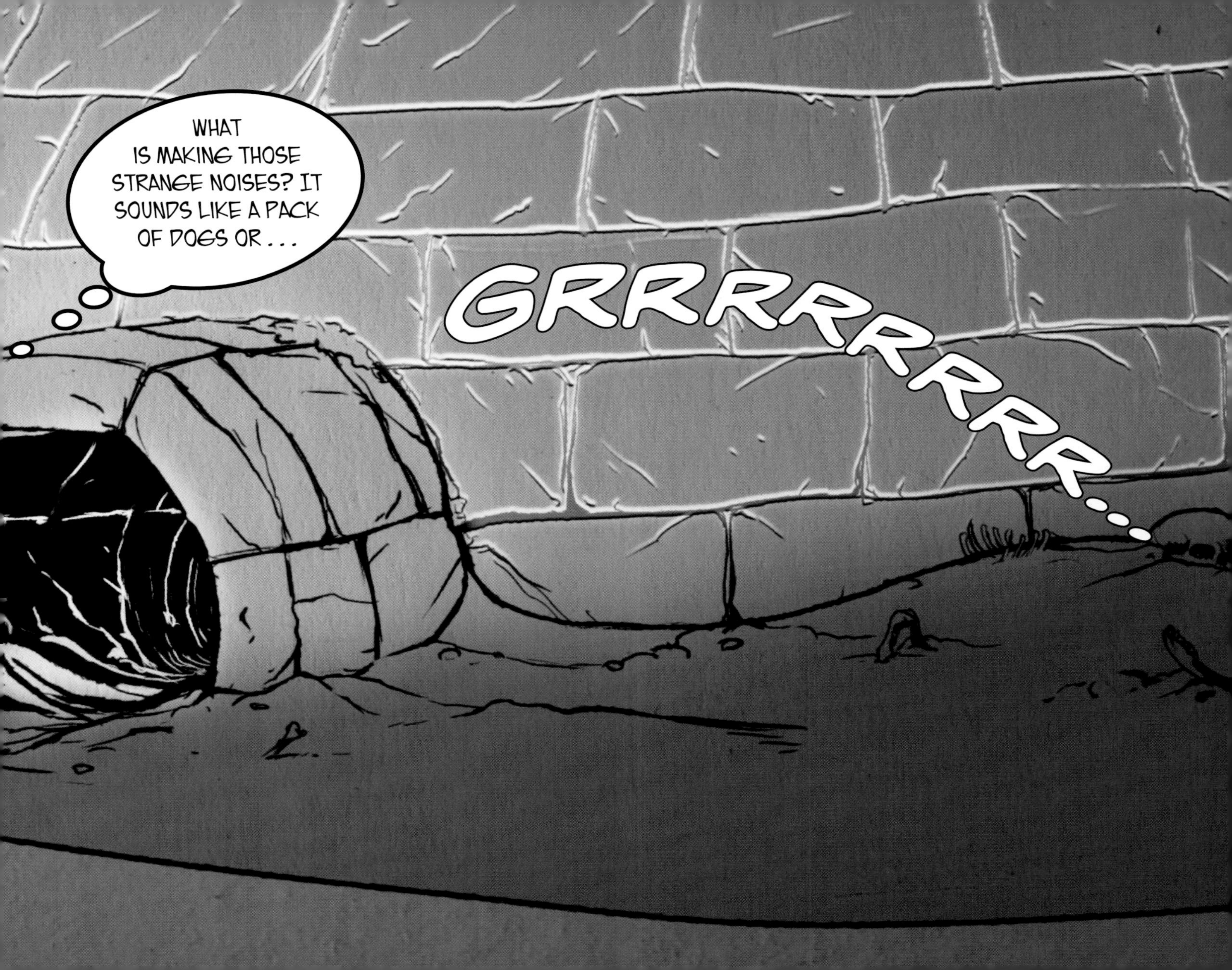
WHAT IS MAKING THOSE STRANGE NOISES? IT SOUNDS LIKE A PACK OF DOGS OR . . .
GRRRRRRRRR....

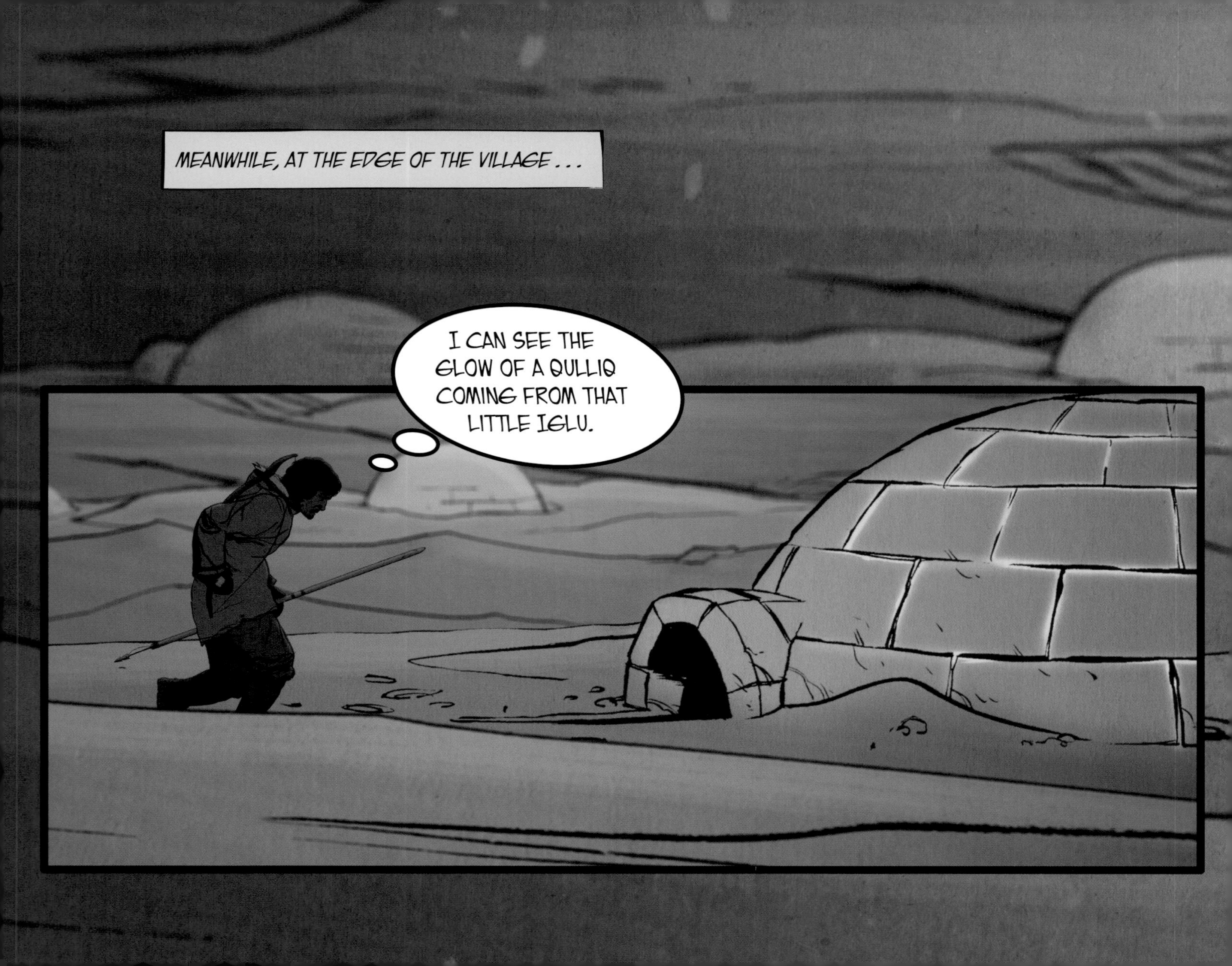
MEANWHILE, AT THE EDGE OF THE VILLAGE . . .
I CAN SEE THE GLOW OF A QULLIQ COMING FROM THAT LITTLE IGLU.

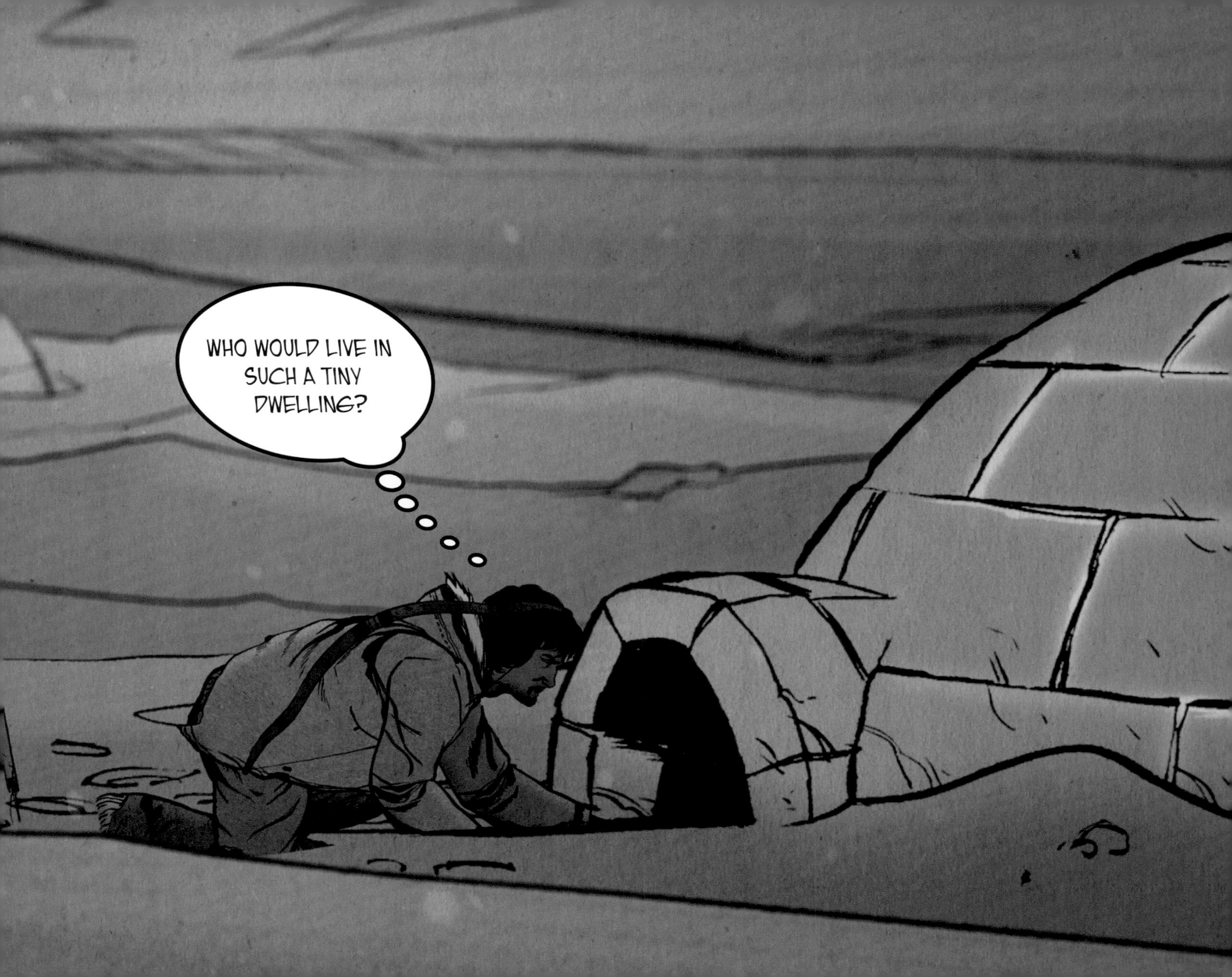
WHO WOULD LIVE IN SUCH A TINY DWELLING?

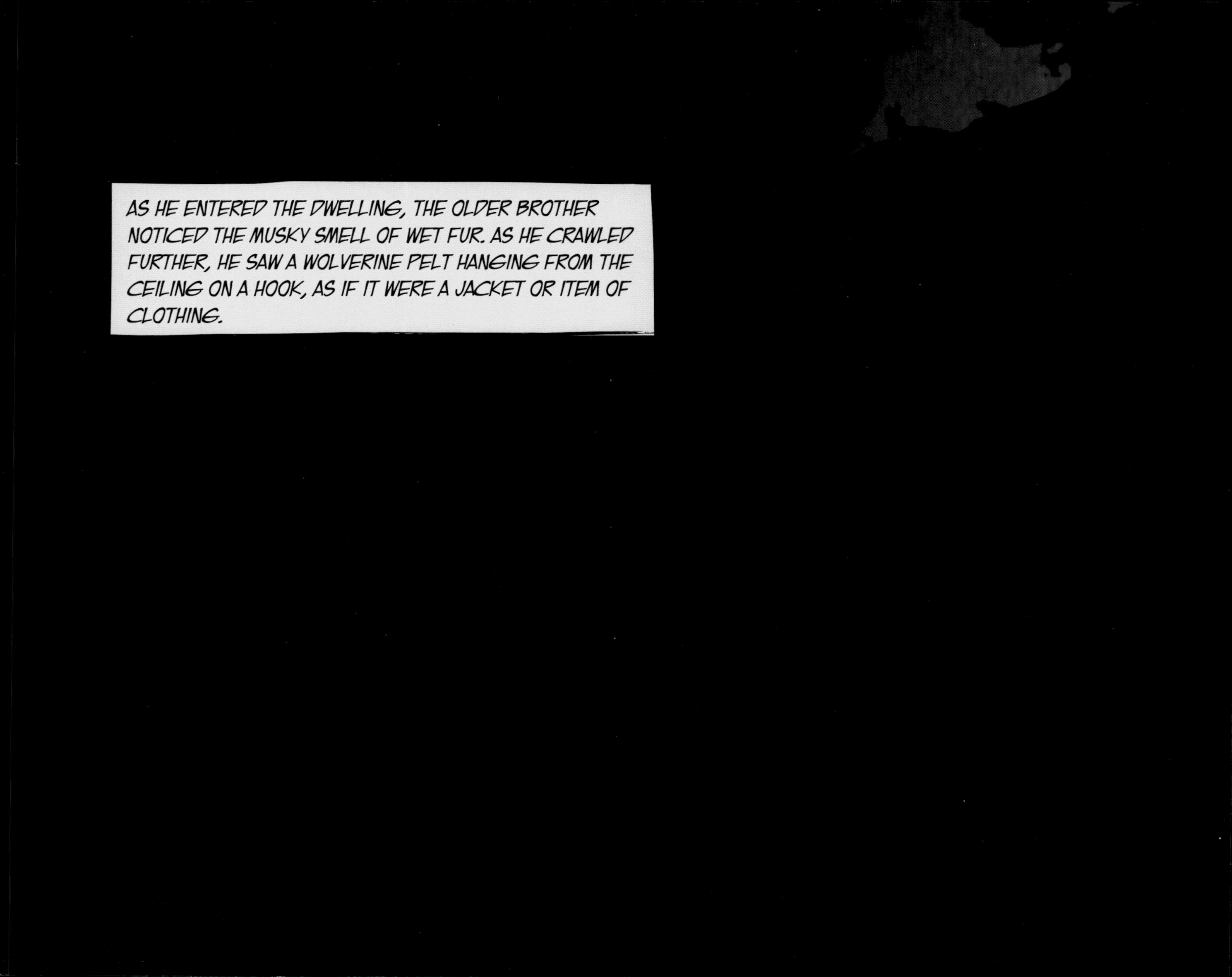
AS HE ENTERED THE DWELLING, THE OLDER BROTHER NOTICED THE MUSKY SMELL OF WET FUR. AS HE CRAWLED FURTHER, HE SAW A WOLVERINE PELT HANGING FROM THE CEILING ON A HOOK, AS IF IT WERE A JACKET OR ITEM OF CLOTHING.

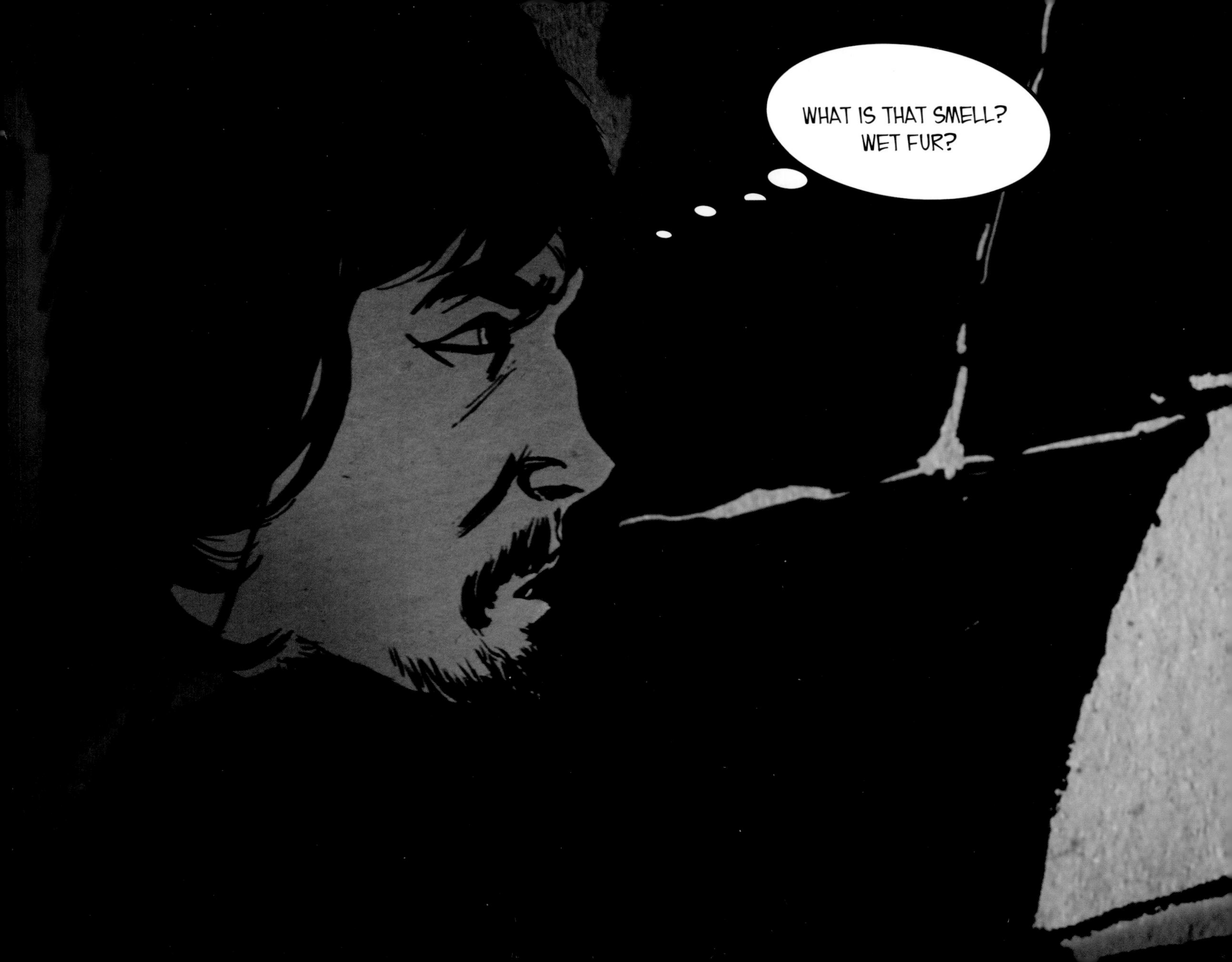
WHAT IS THAT SMELL?
WET FUR?

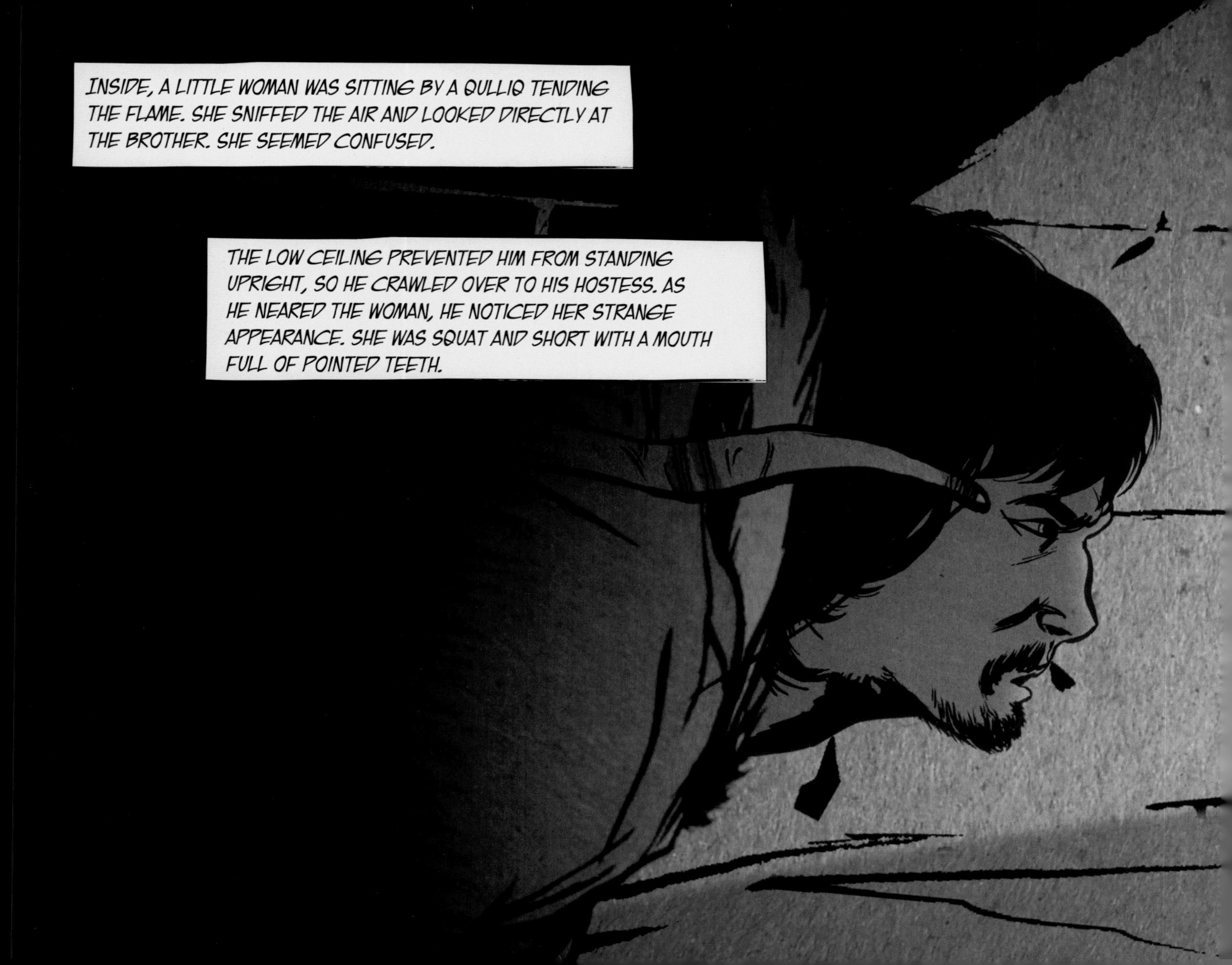
INSIDE, A LITTLE WOMAN WAS SITTING BY A QULLIQ TENDING THE FLAME. SHE SNIFFED THE AIR AND LOOKED DIRECTLY AT THE BROTHER. SHE SEEMED CONFUSED.
THE LOW CEILING PREVENTED HIM FROM STANDING UPRIGHT, SO HE CRAWLED OVER TO HIS HOSTESS. AS HE NEARED THE WOMAN, HE NOTICED HER STRANGE APPEARANCE. SHE WAS SQUAT AND SHORT WITH A MOUTH FULL OF POINTED TEETH.

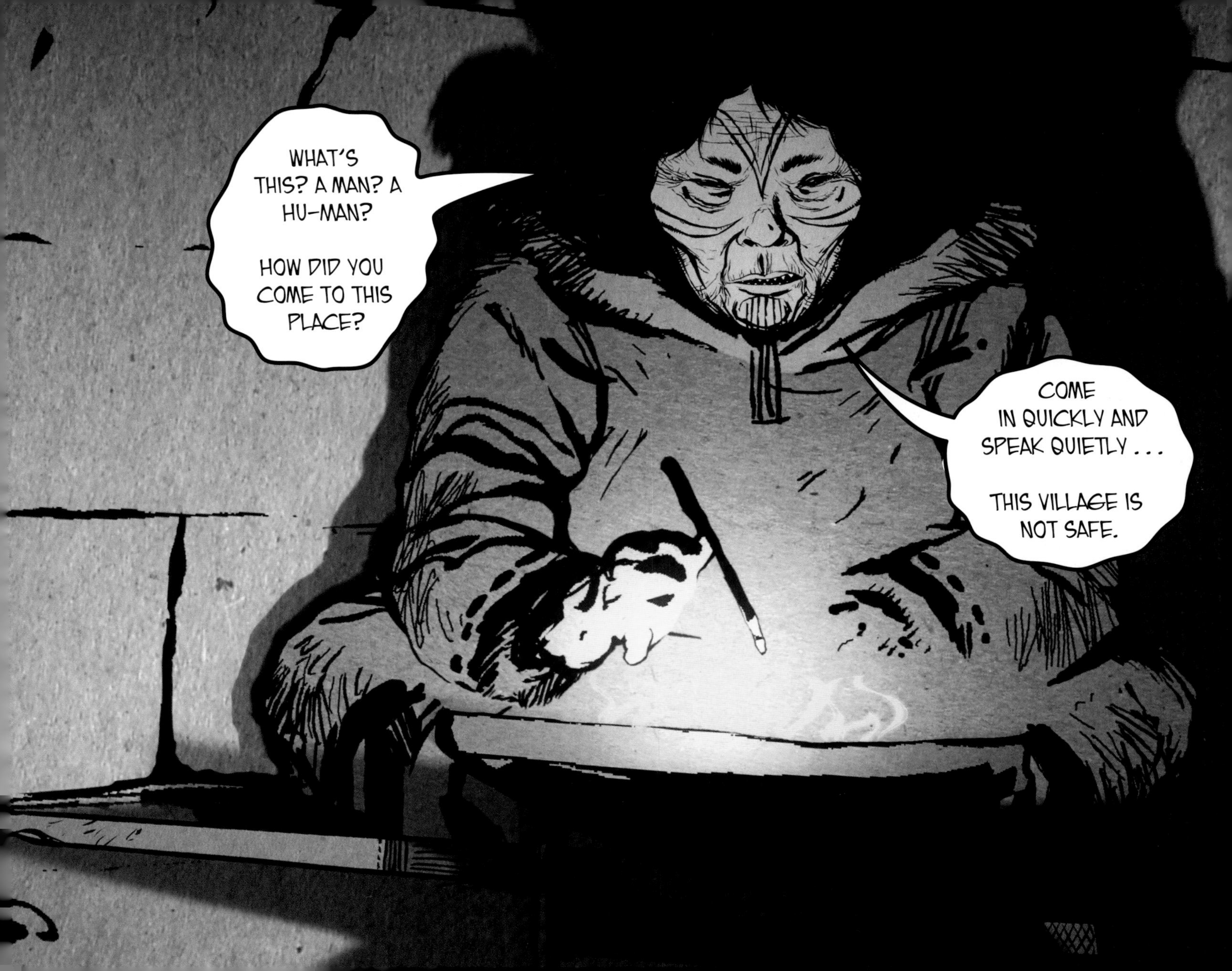
WHAT'S THIS? A MAN? A HU-MAN?
HOW DID YOU COME TO THIS PLACE?
COME IN QUICKLY AND SPEAK QUIETLY . . .
THIS VILLAGE IS NOT SAFE.

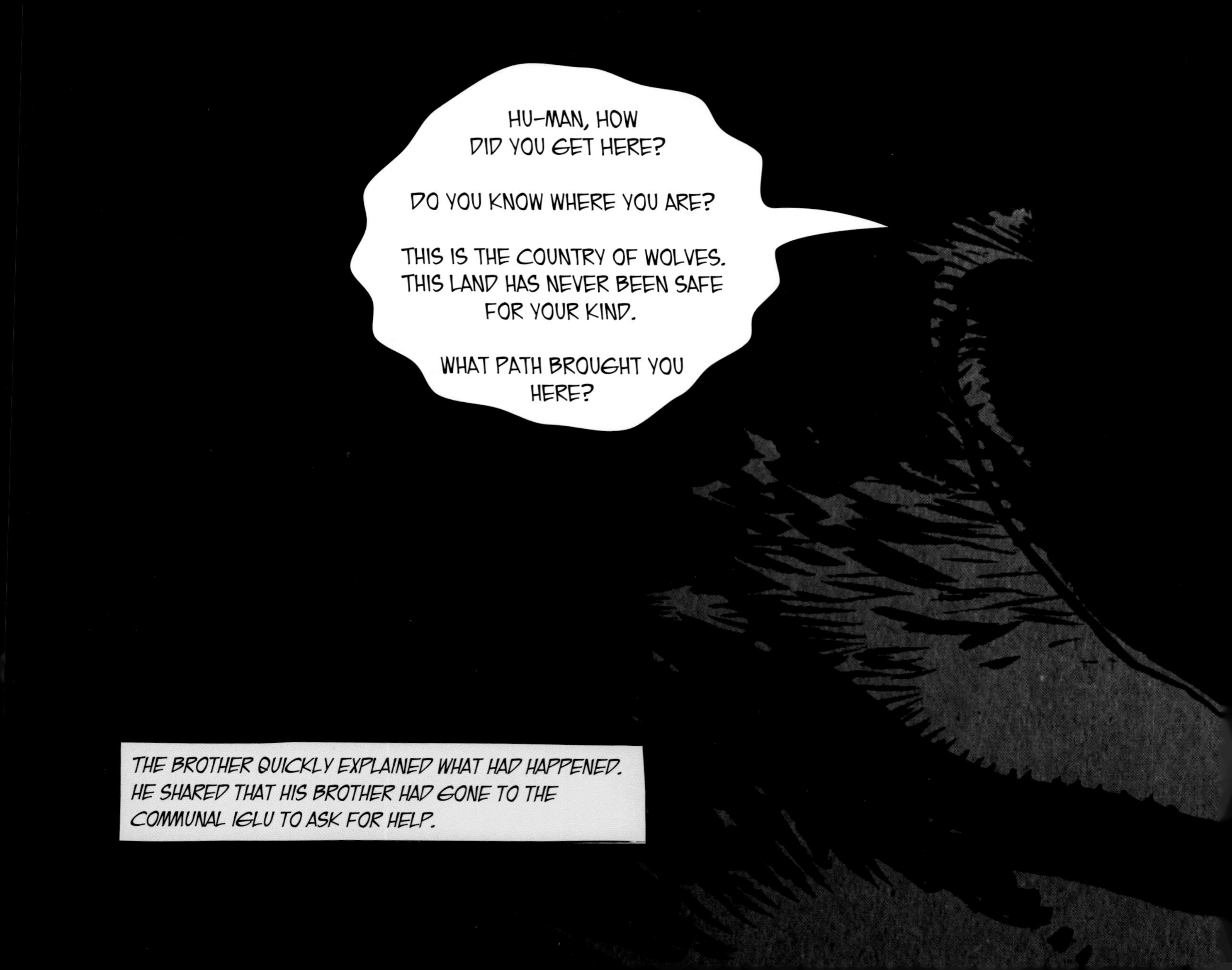
HU-MAN, HOW DID YOU GET HERE?
DO YOU KNOW WHERE YOU ARE?
THIS IS THE COUNTRY OF WOLVES. THIS LAND HAS NEVER BEEN SAFE FOR YOUR KIND.
WHAT PATH BROUGHT YOU HERE?
THE BROTHER QUICKLY EXPLAINED WHAT HAD HAPPENED. HE SHARED THAT HIS BROTHER HAD GONE TO THE COMMUNAL IGLU TO ASK FOR HELP.

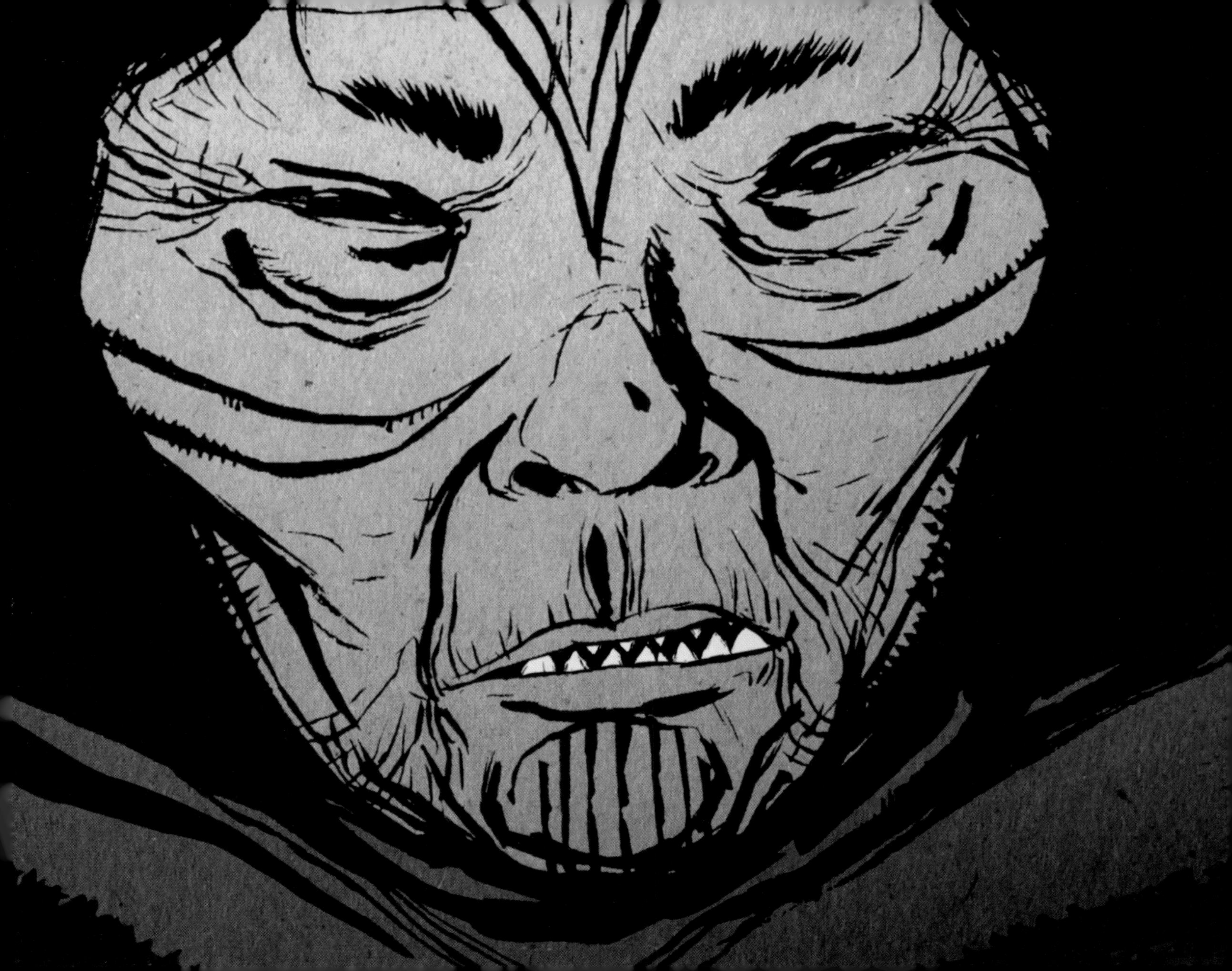

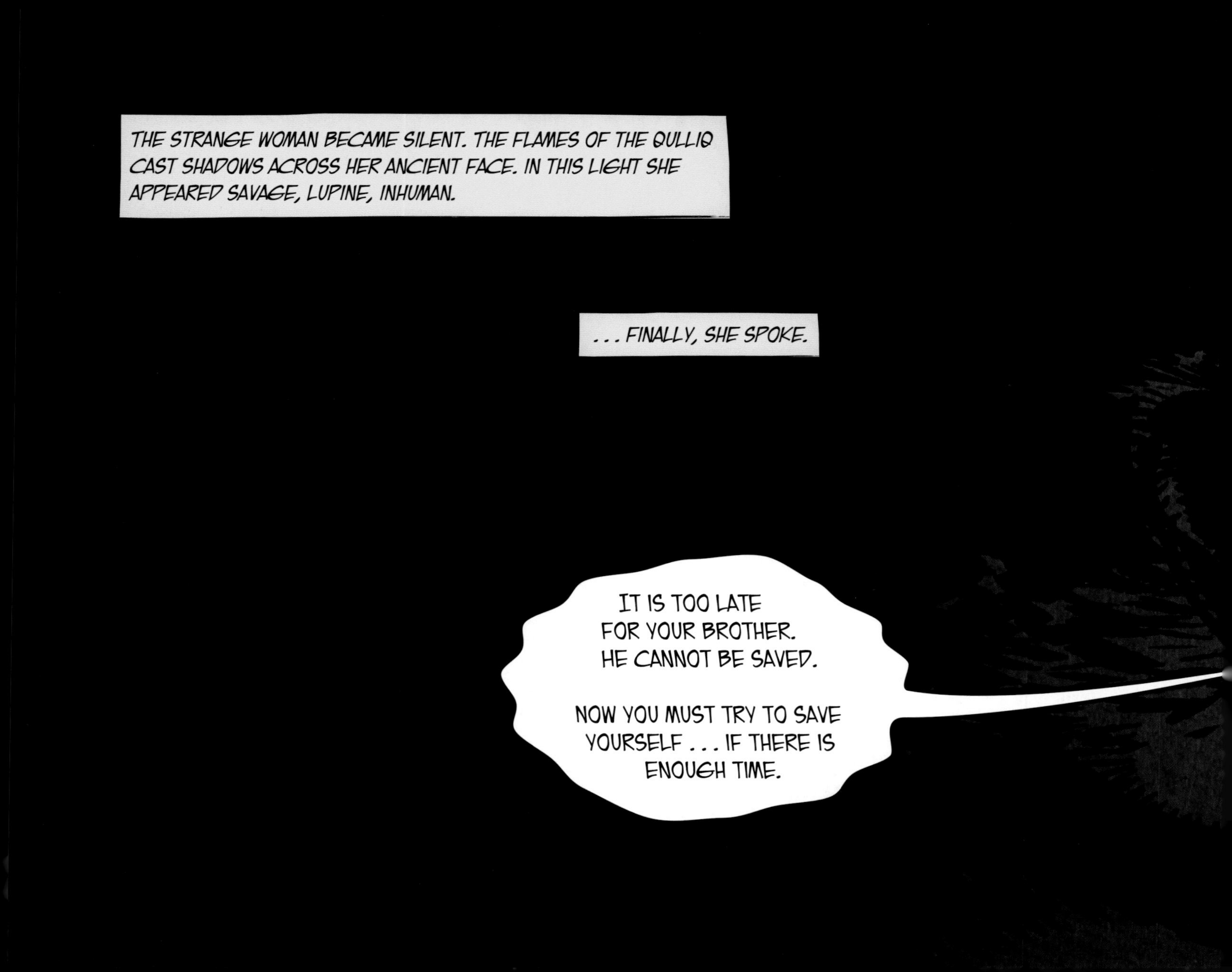
THE STRANGE WOMAN BECAME SILENT. THE FLAMES OF THE QULLIQ CAST SHADOWS ACROSS HER ANCIENT FACE. IN THIS LIGHT SHE APPEARED SAVAGE, LUPINE, INHUMAN.
. . . FINALLY, SHE SPOKE.
IT IS TOO LATE FOR YOUR BROTHER. HE CANNOT BE SAVED. NOW YOU MUST TRY TO SAVE YOURSELF . . . IF THERE IS ENOUGH TIME.

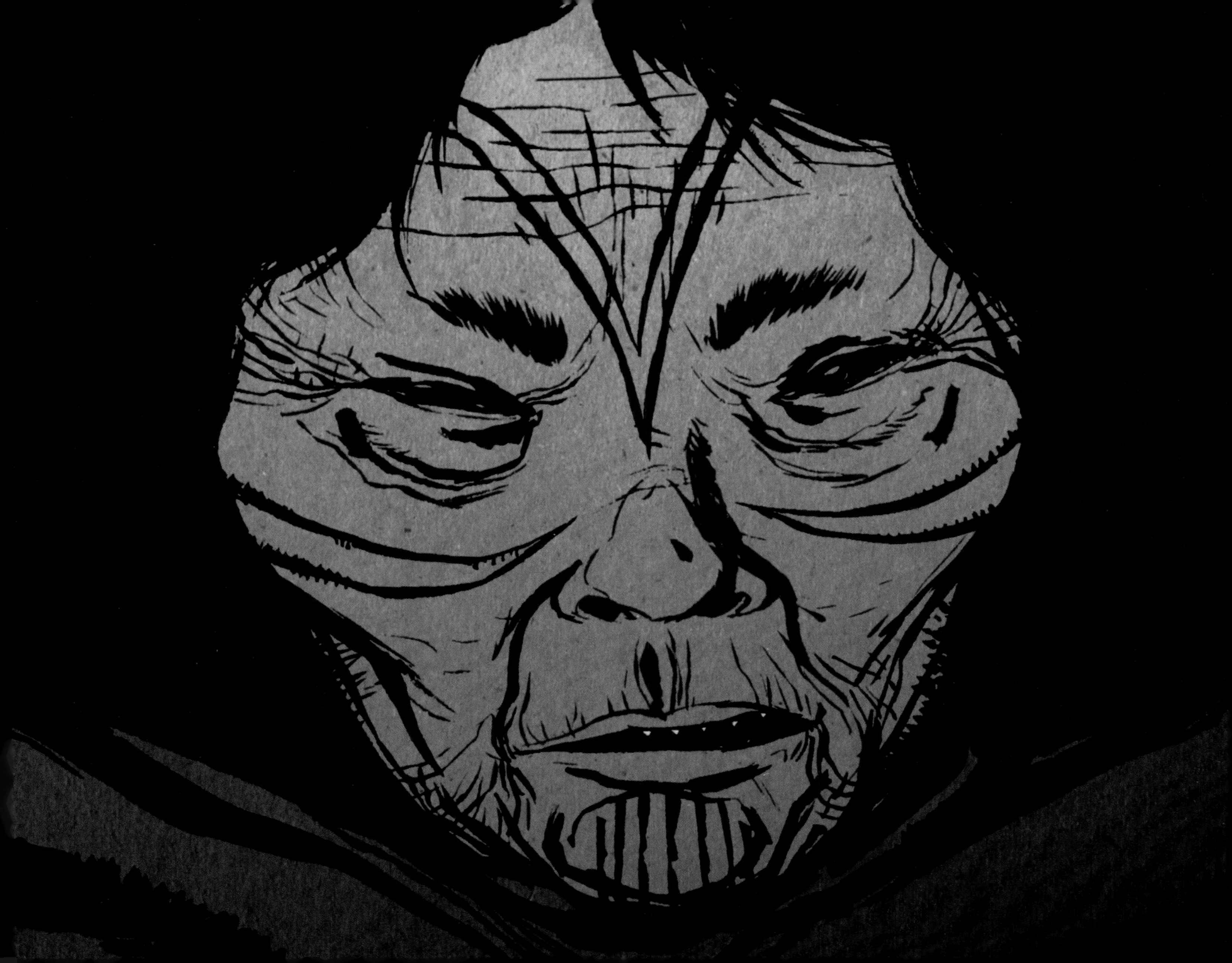

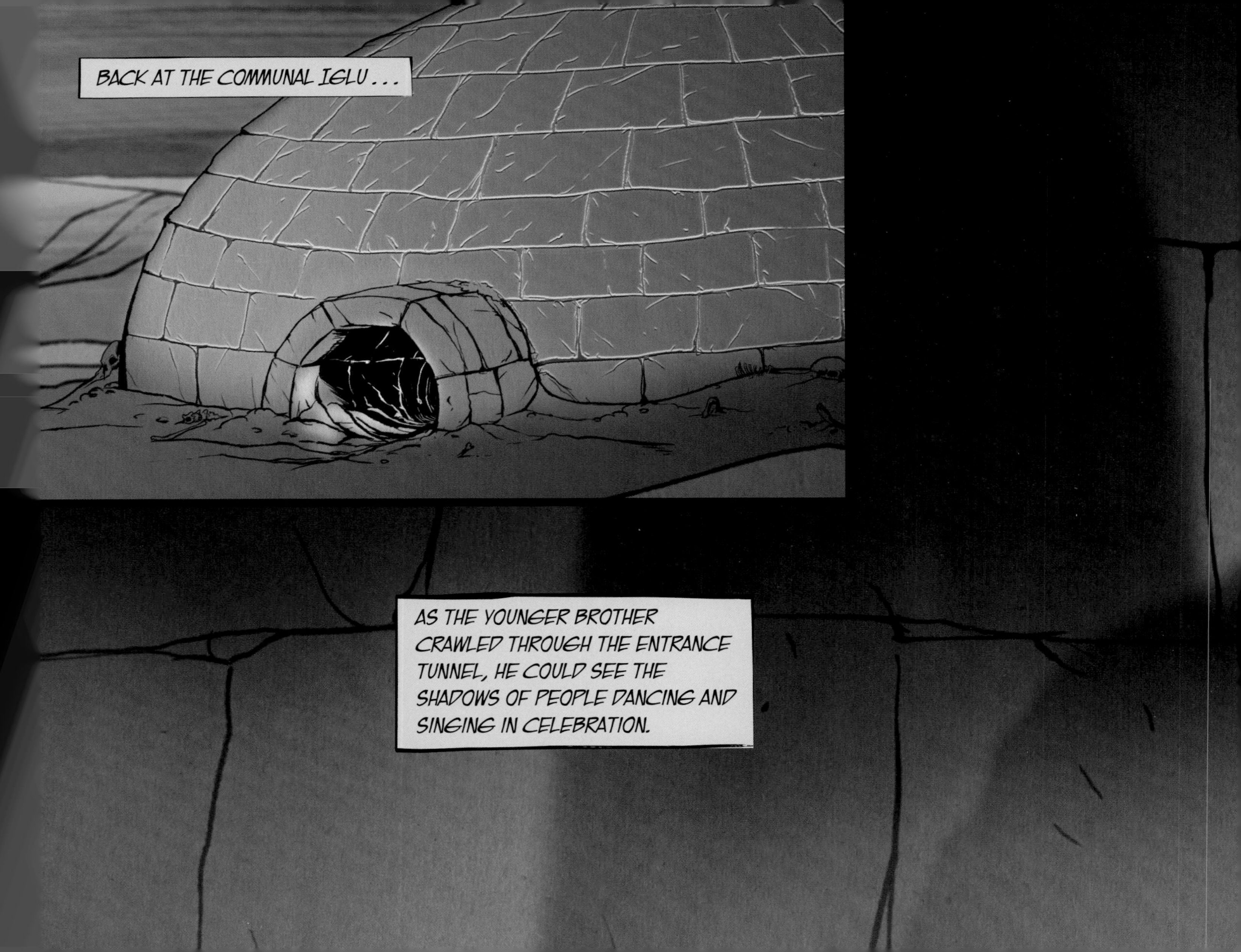
BACK AT THE COMMUNAL IGLU . . .
AS THE YOUNGER BROTHER CRAWLED THROUGH THE ENTRANCE TUNNEL, HE COULD SEE THE SHADOWS OF PEOPLE DANCING AND SINGING IN CELEBRATION.

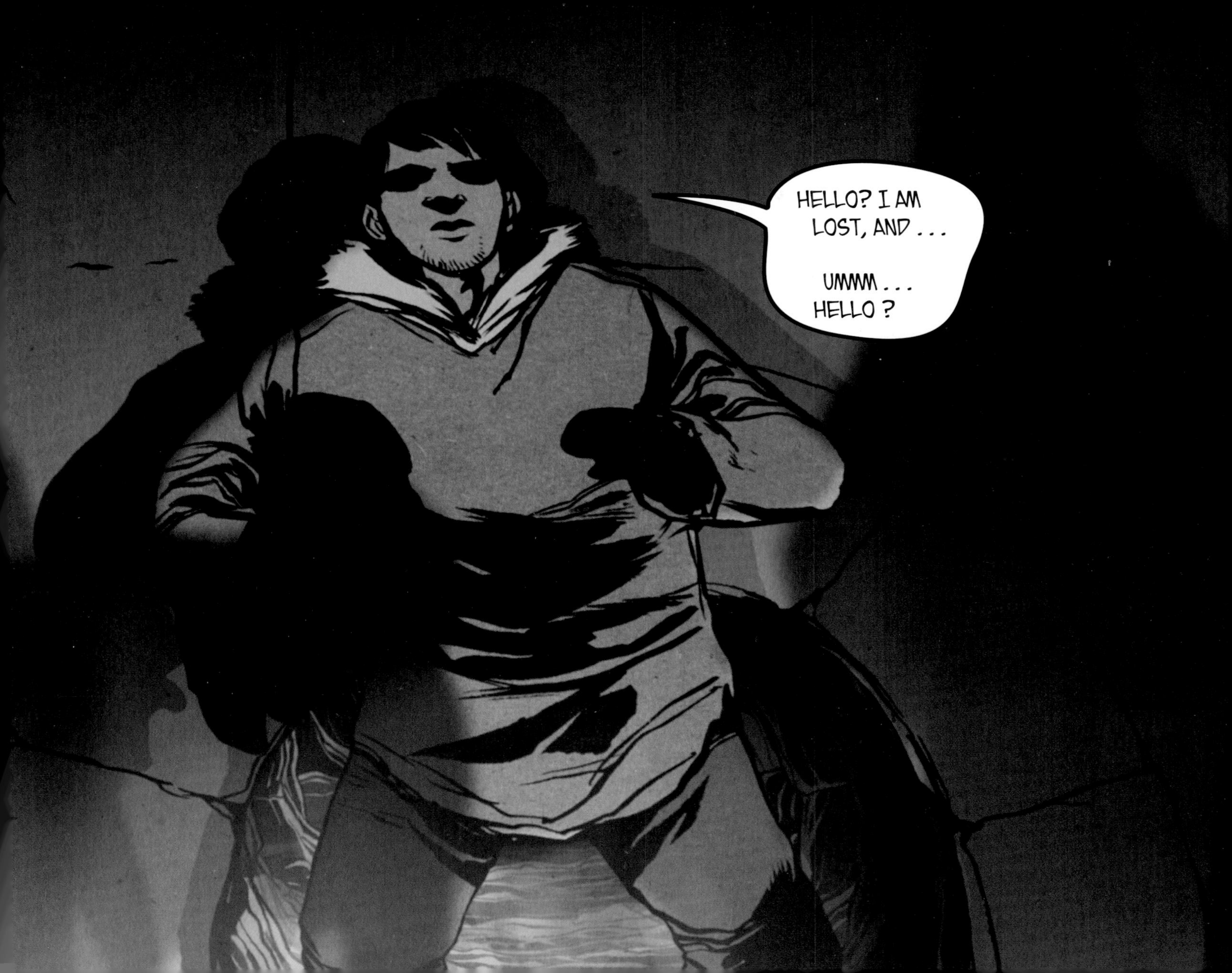
HELLO? I AM LOST, AND . . .
UMMM . . . HELLO ?

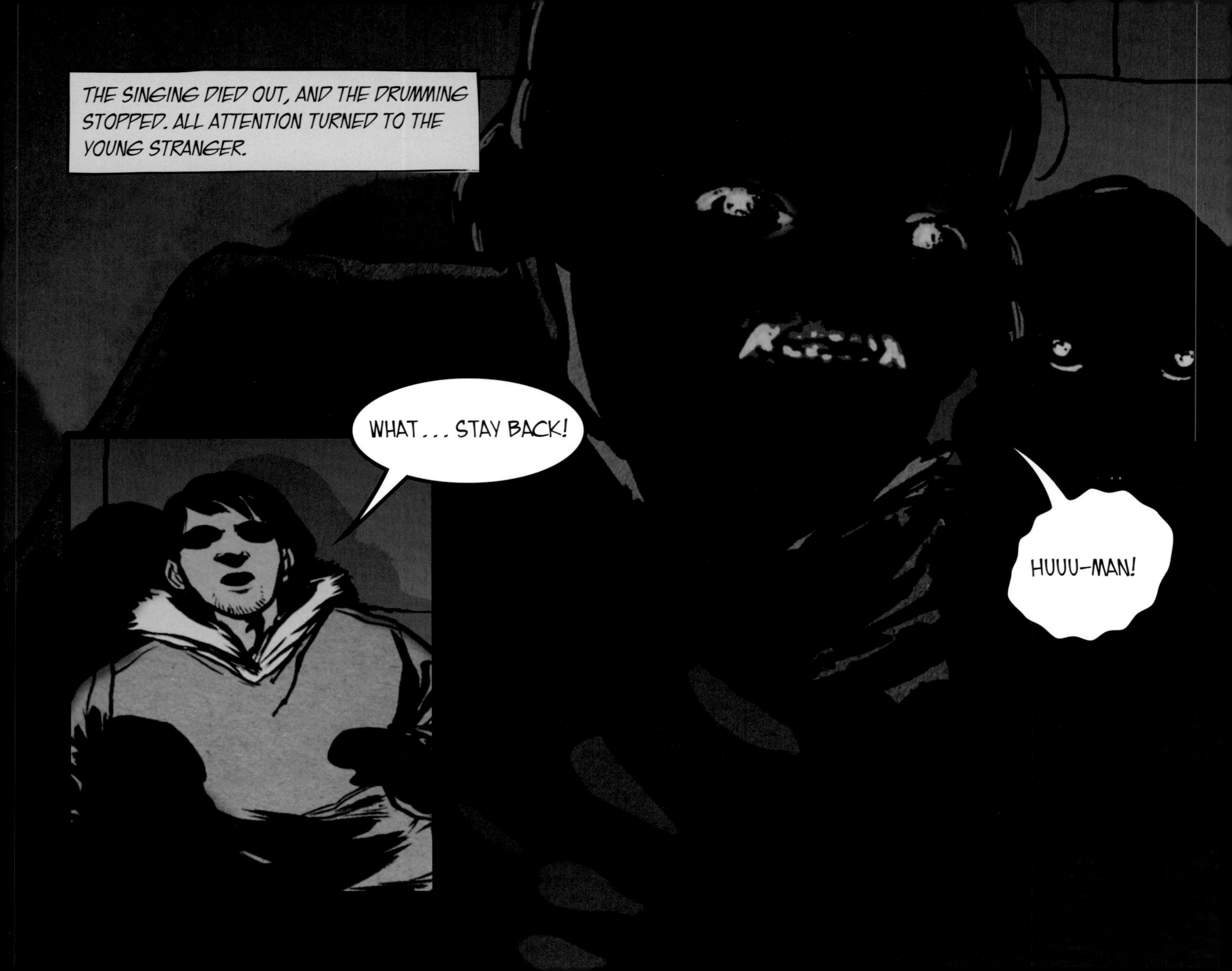
THE SINGING DIED OUT, AND THE DRUMMING STOPPED. ALL ATTENTION TURNED TO THE YOUNG STRANGER.
WHAT . . . STAY BACK!
HUUU-MAN!

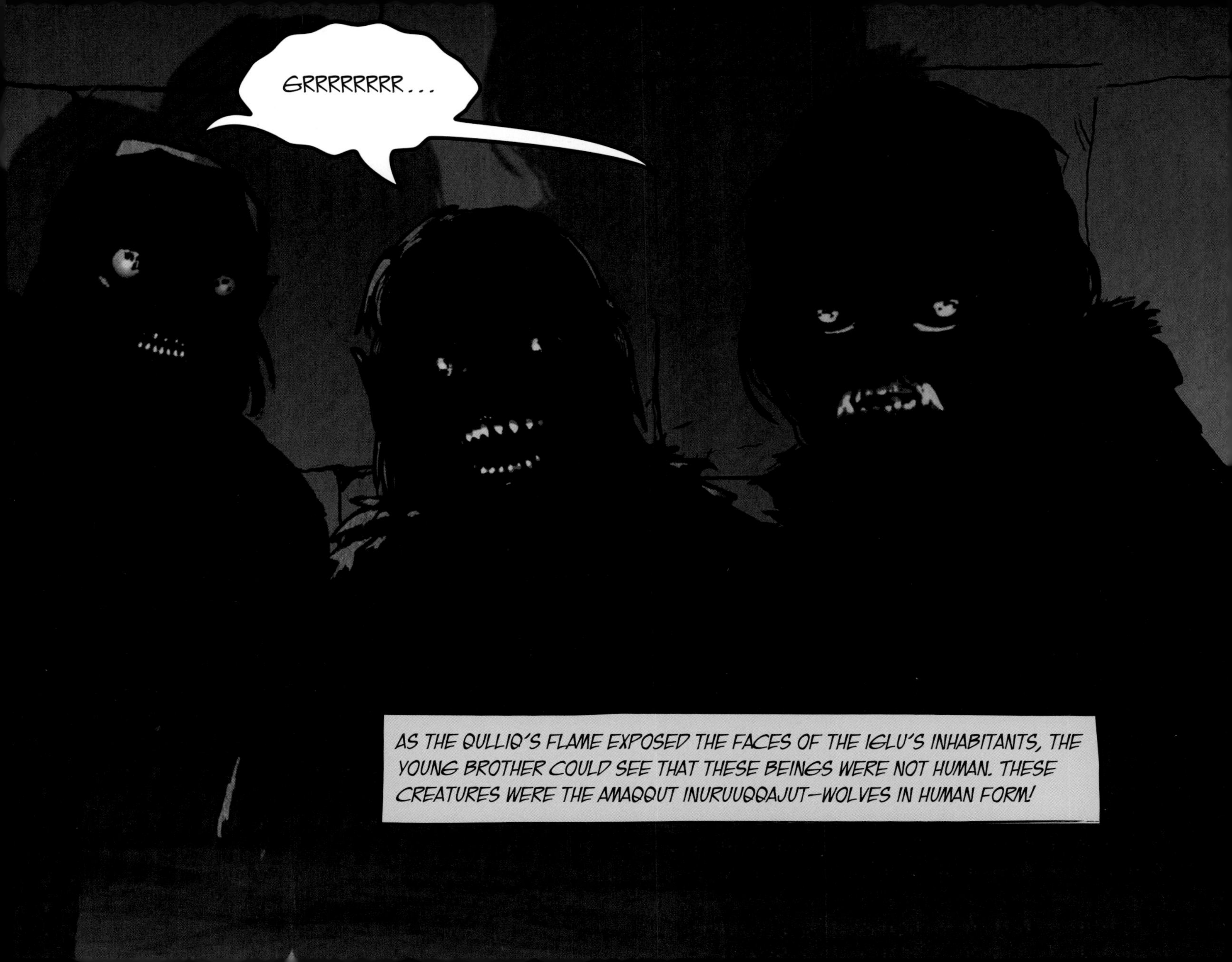
GRRRRRRRR...
AS THE QULLIQ'S FLAME EXPOSED THE FACES OF THE IGLU'S INHABITANTS, THE YOUNG BROTHER COULD SEE THAT THESE BEINGS WERE NOT HUMAN. THESE CREATURES WERE THE AMAQQUT INURUUQQAJUT—WOLVES IN HUMAN FORM!

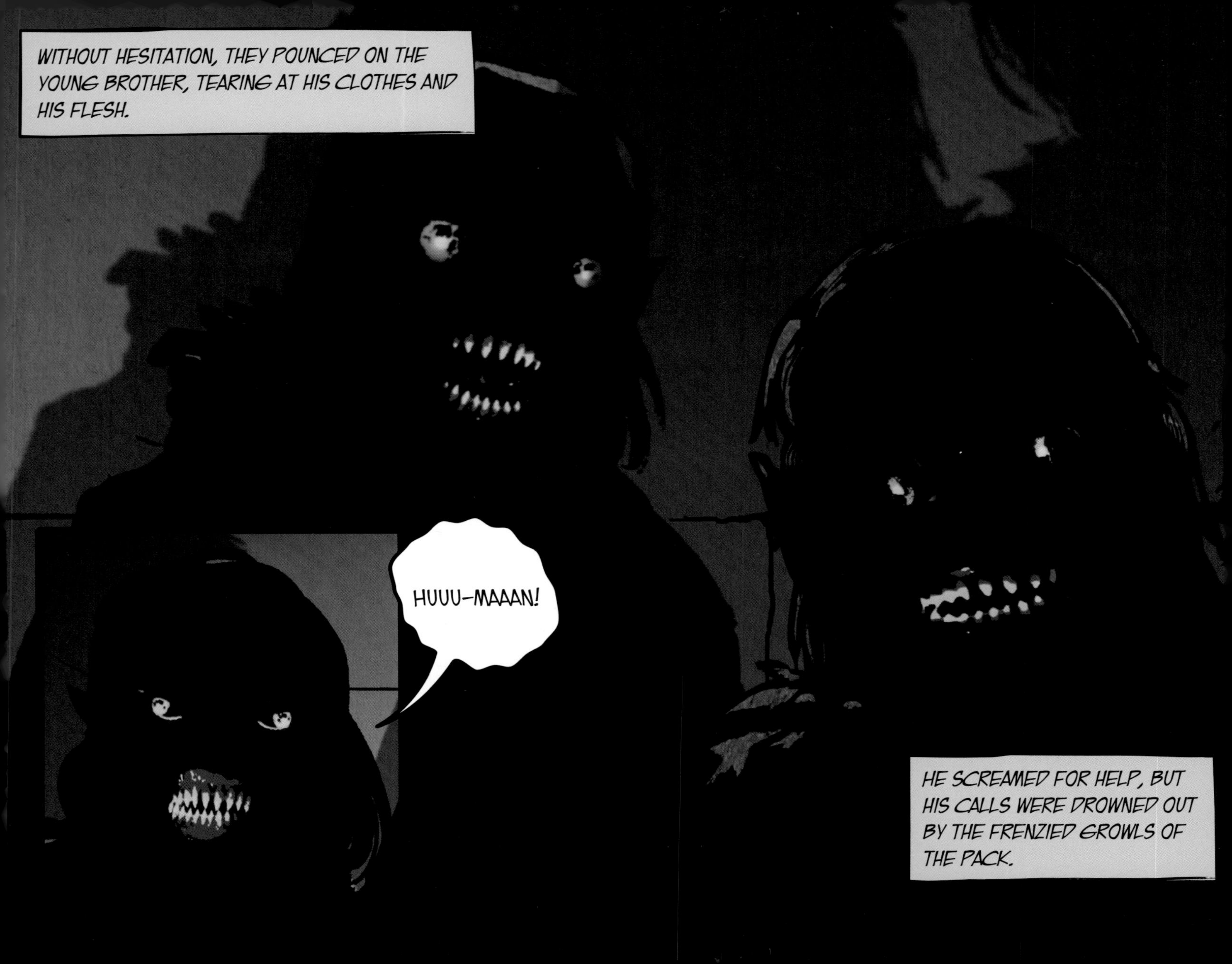
WITHOUT HESITATION, THEY POUNCED ON THE YOUNG BROTHER, TEARING AT HIS CLOTHES AND HIS FLESH.
HUUU-MAAAN!
HE SCREAMED FOR HELP, BUT HIS CALLS WERE DROWNED OUT BY THE FRENZIED GROWLS OF THE PACK.

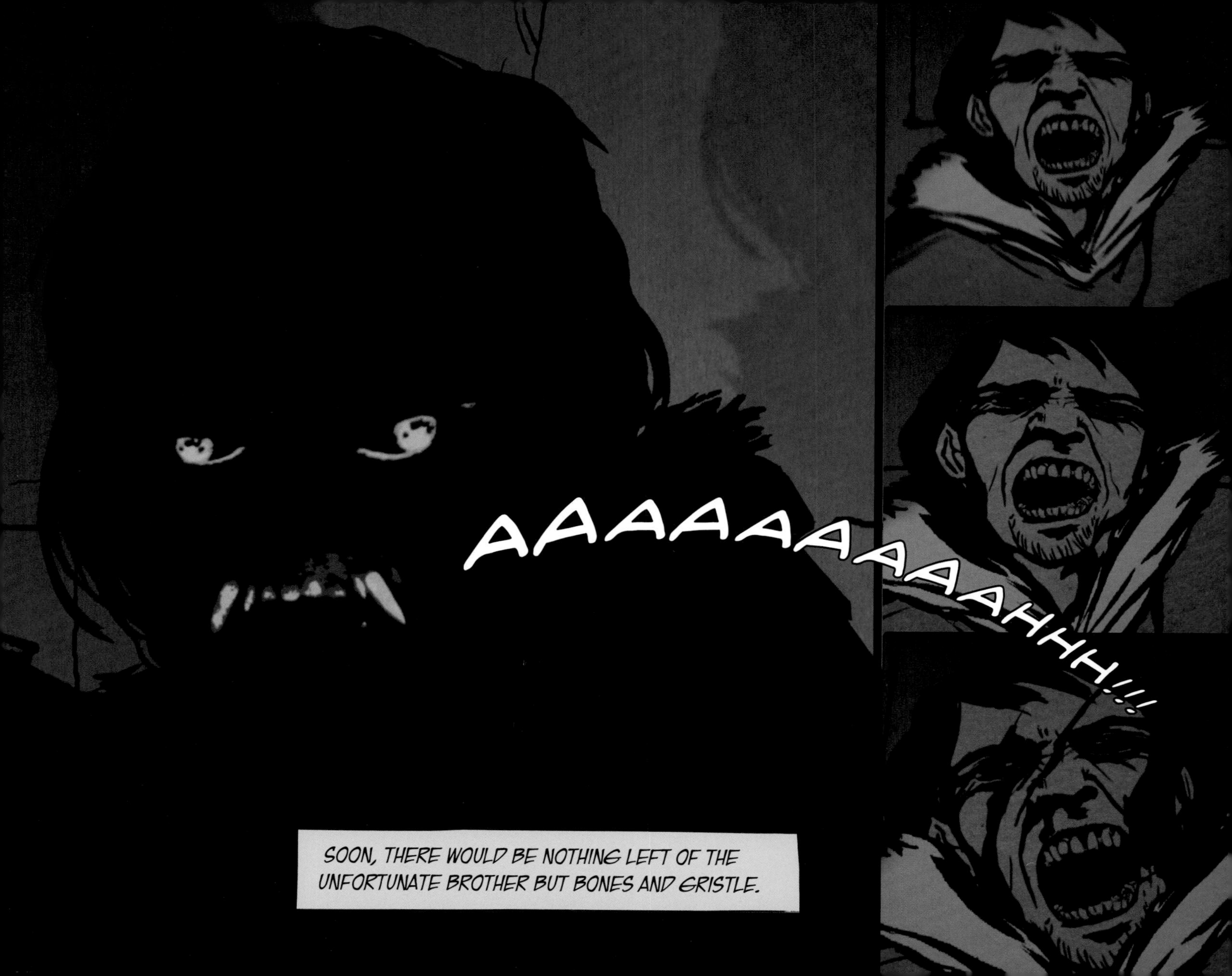
AAAAAAAAAAAHHH!!!!
SOON, THERE WOULD BE NOTHING LEFT OF THE UNFORTUNATE BROTHER BUT BONES AND GRISTLE.

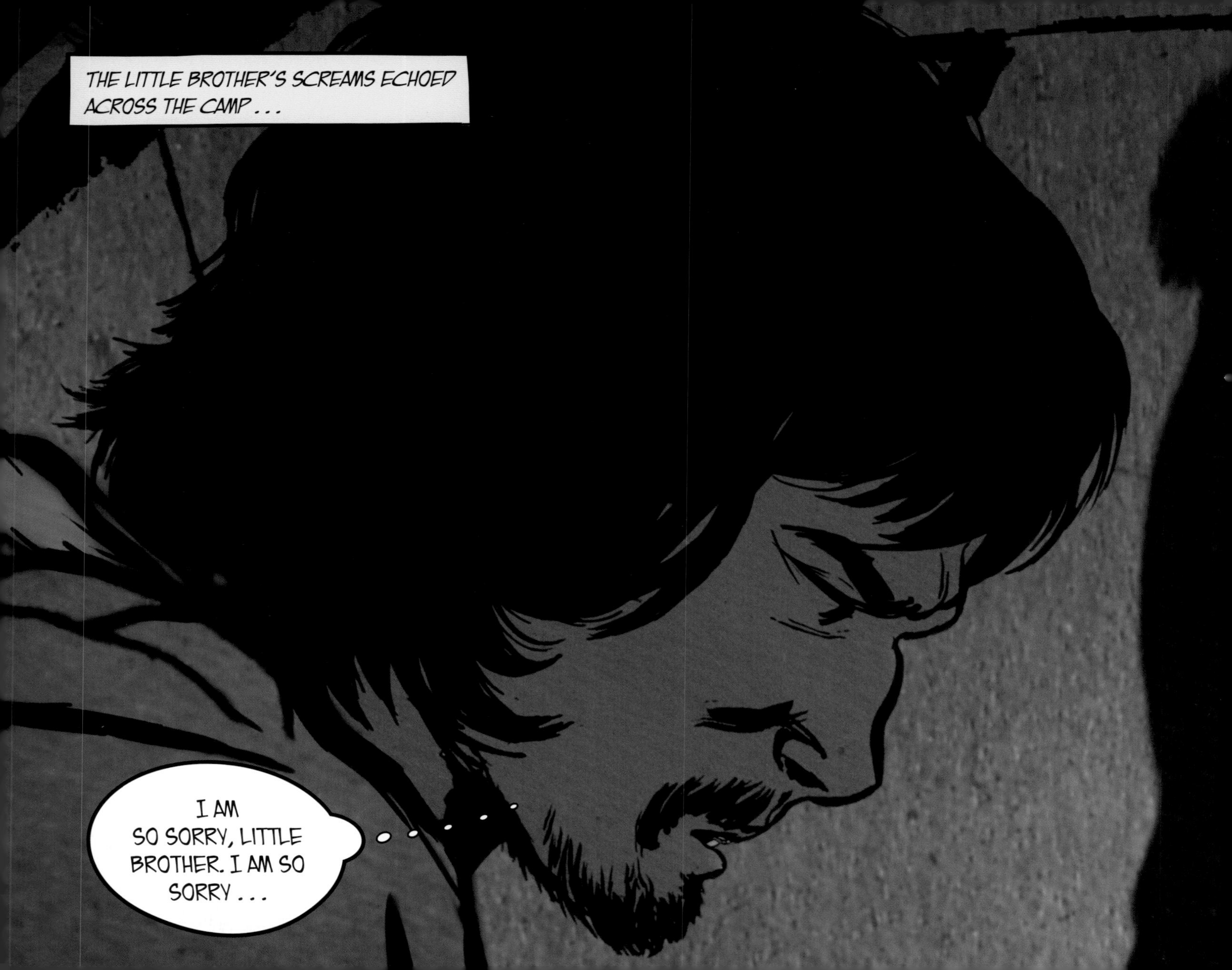
THE LITTLE BROTHER'S SCREAMS ECHOED ACROSS THE CAMP . . .
I AM SO SORRY, LITTLE BROTHER. I AM SO SORRY . . .

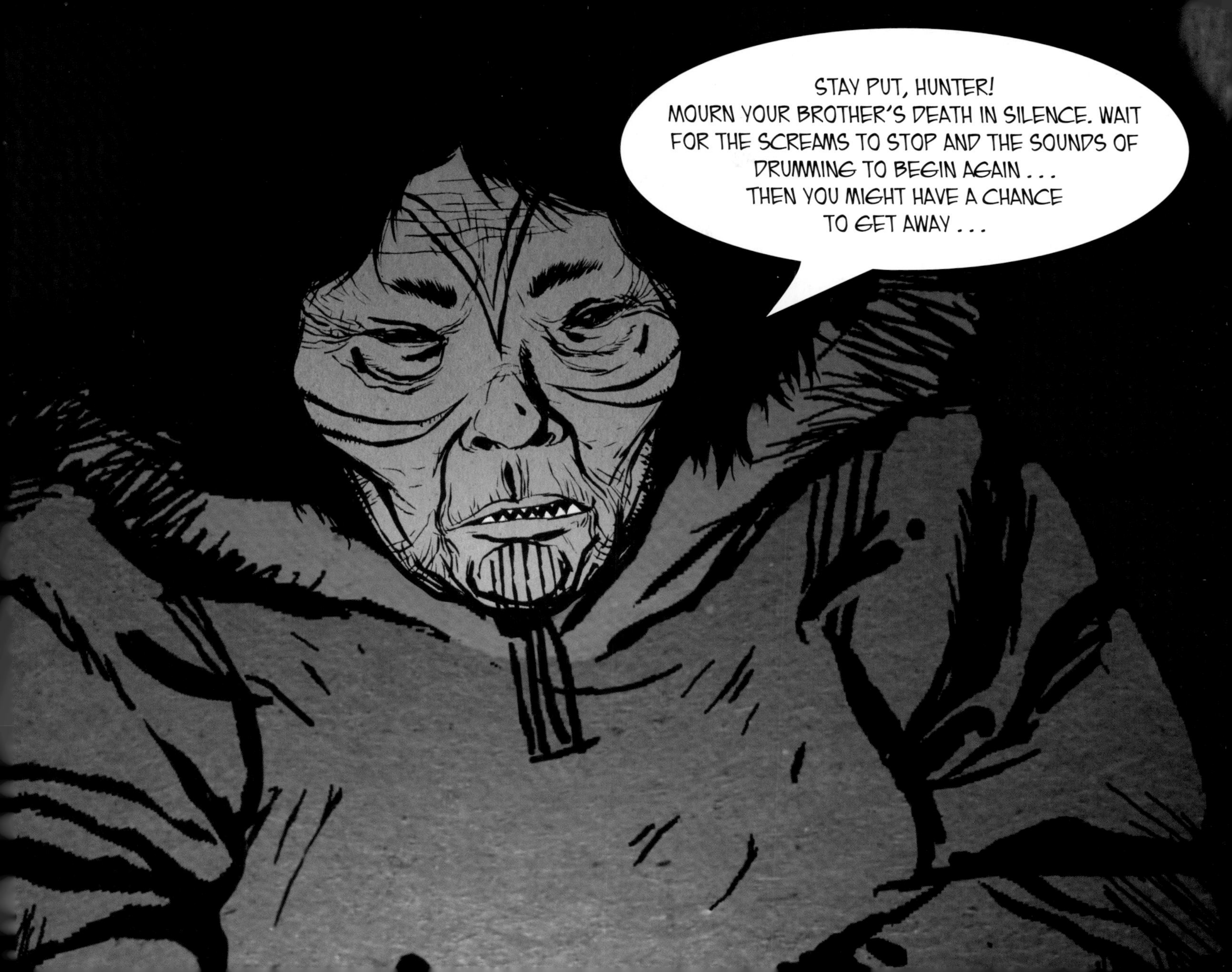
STAY PUT, HUNTER! MOURN YOUR BROTHER'S DEATH IN SILENCE. WAIT FOR THE SCREAMS TO STOP AND THE SOUNDS OF DRUMMING TO BEGIN AGAIN . . . THEN YOU MIGHT HAVE A CHANCE TO GET AWAY . . .

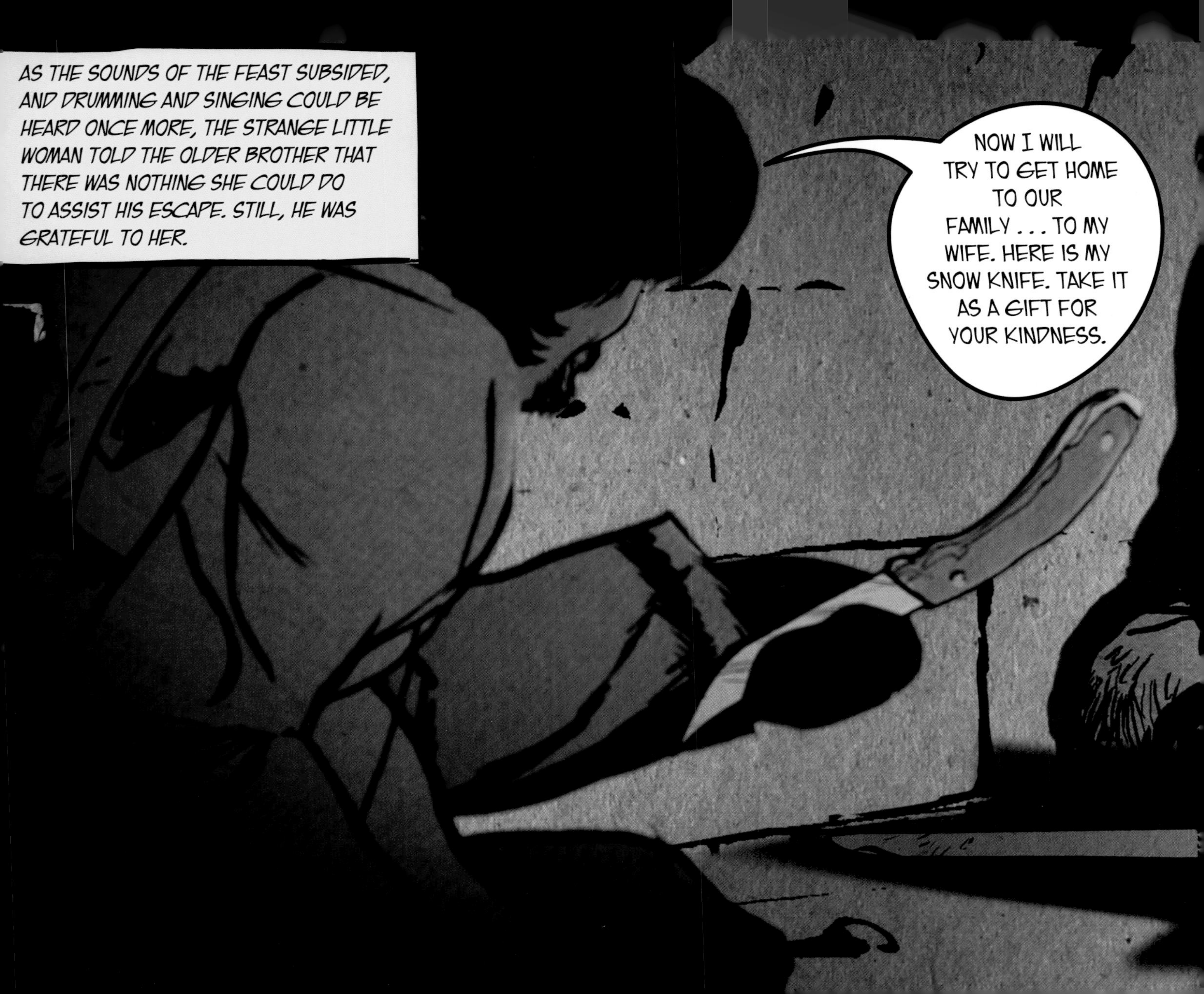
AS THE SOUNDS OF THE FEAST SUBSIDED, AND DRUMMING AND SINGING COULD BE HEARD ONCE MORE, THE STRANGE LITTLE WOMAN TOLD THE OLDER BROTHER THAT THERE WAS NOTHING SHE COULD DO TO ASSIST HIS ESCAPE. STILL, HE WAS GRATEFUL TO HER.
NOW I WILL TRY TO GET HOME TO OUR FAMILY . . . TO MY WIFE. HERE IS MY SNOW KNIFE. TAKE IT AS A GIFT FOR YOUR KINDNESS.

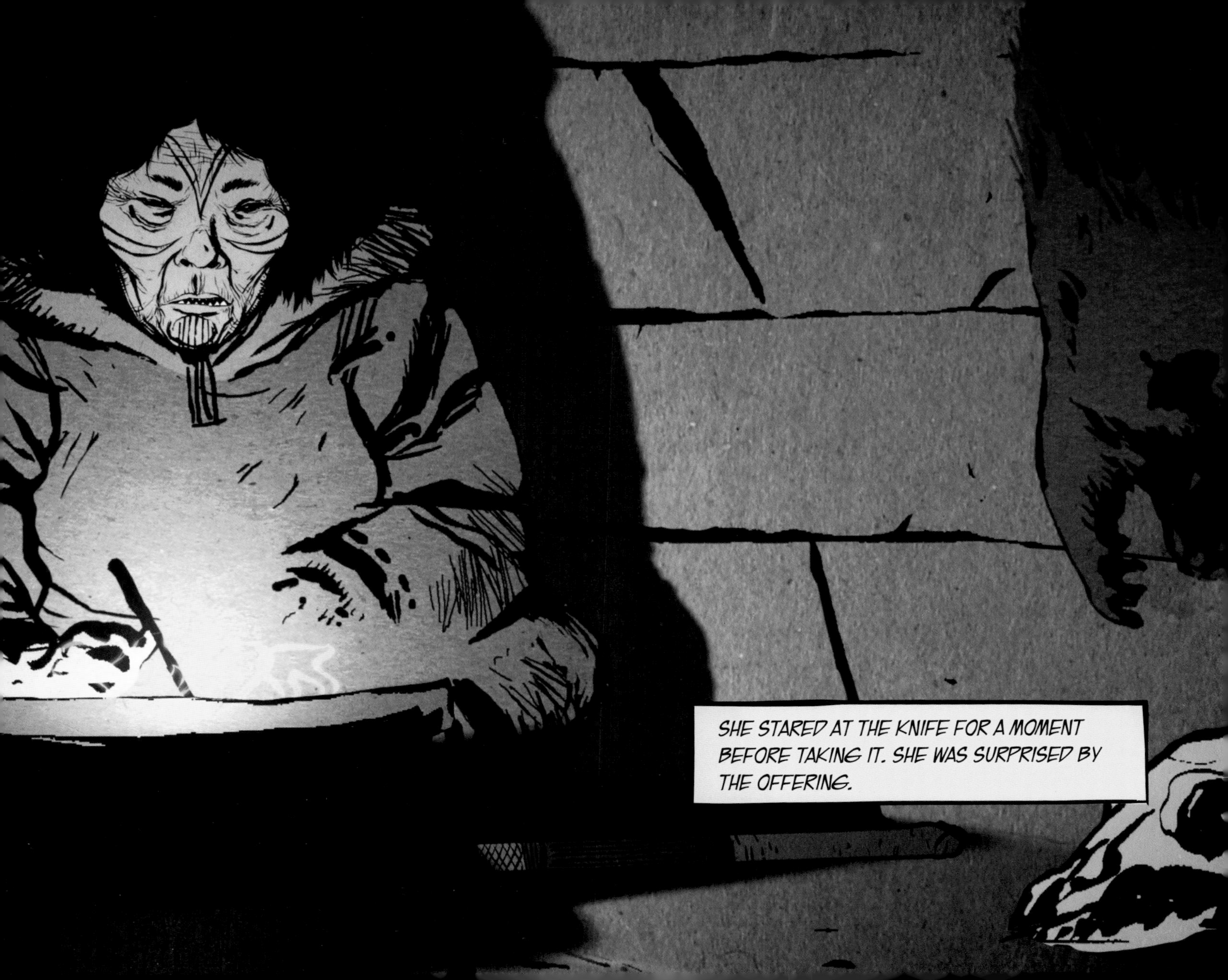
SHE STARED AT THE KNIFE FOR A MOMENT BEFORE TAKING IT. SHE WAS SURPRISED BY THE OFFERING.

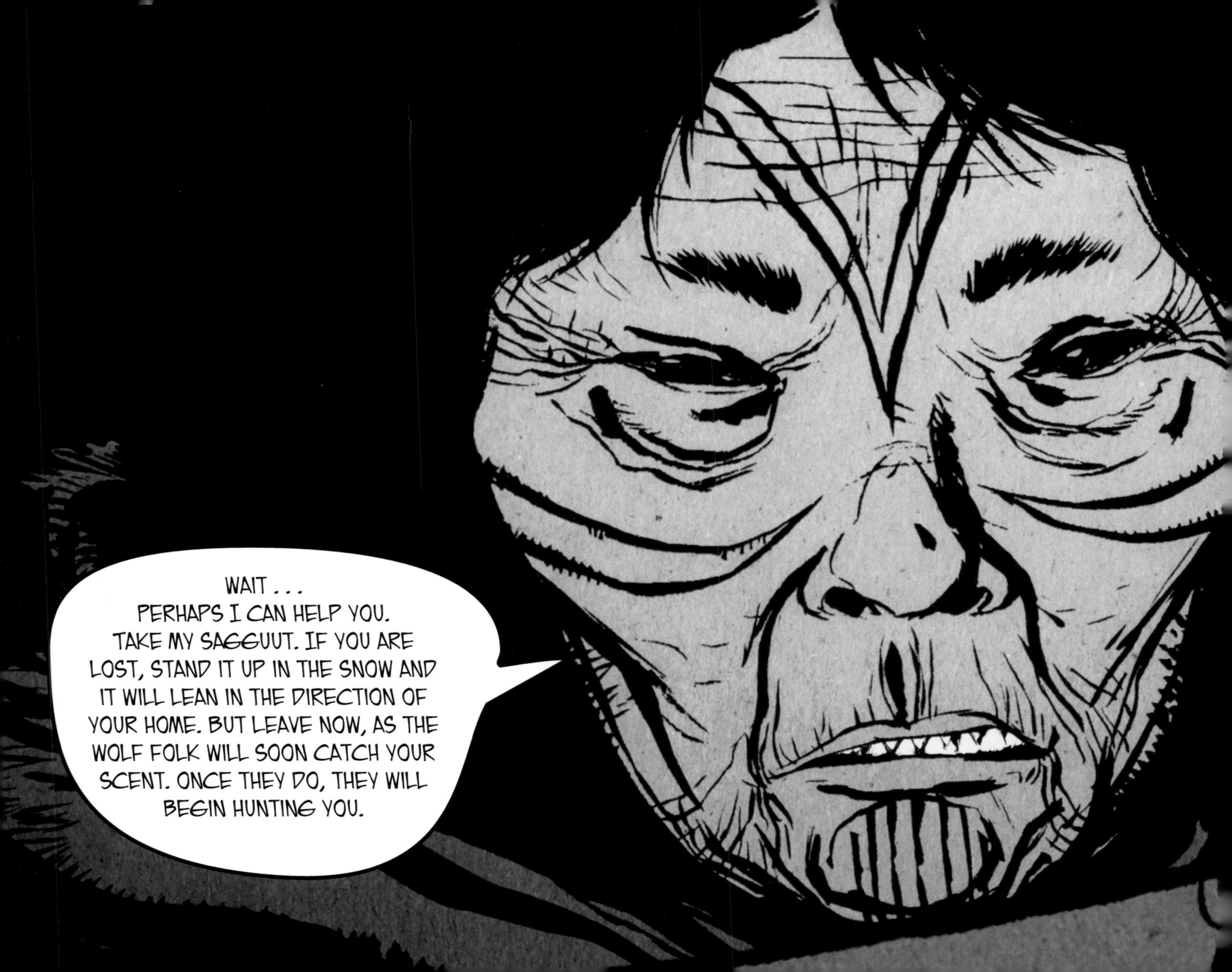
WAIT . . . PERHAPS I CAN HELP YOU. TAKE MY SAGGUUT. IF YOU ARE LOST, STAND IT UP IN THE SNOW AND IT WILL LEAN IN THE DIRECTION OF YOUR HOME. BUT LEAVE NOW, AS THE WOLF FOLK WILL SOON CATCH YOUR SCENT. ONCE THEY DO, THEY WILL BEGIN HUNTING YOU.

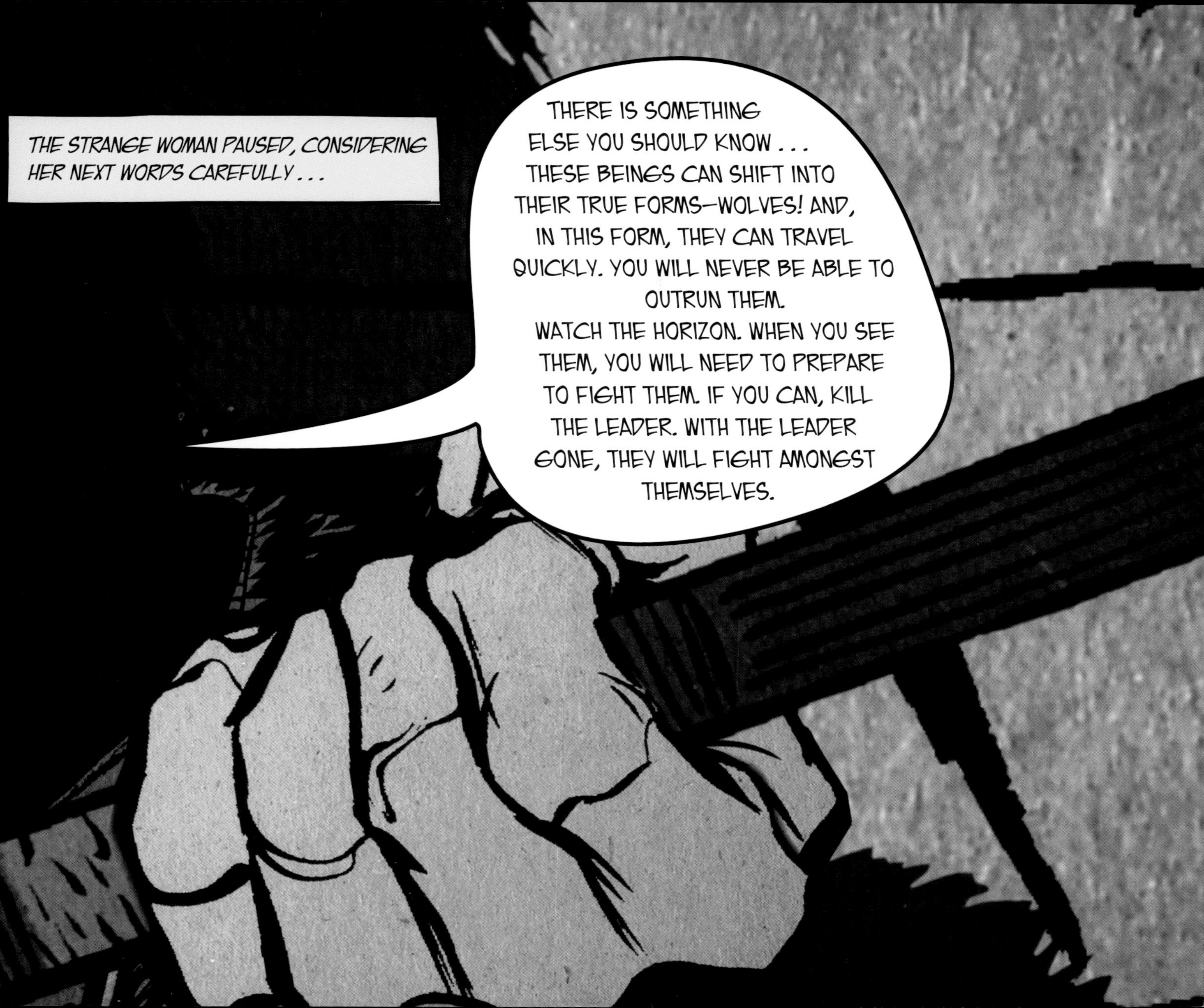
THE STRANGE WOMAN PAUSED, CONSIDERING HER NEXT WORDS CAREFULLY . . .
THERE IS SOMETHING ELSE YOU SHOULD KNOW . . . THESE BEINGS CAN SHIFT INTO THEIR TRUE FORMS—WOLVES! AND, IN THIS FORM, THEY CAN TRAVEL QUICKLY. YOU WILL NEVER BE ABLE TO OUTRUN THEM. WATCH THE HORIZON. WHEN YOU SEE THEM, YOU WILL NEED TO PREPARE TO FIGHT THEM. IF YOU CAN, KILL THE LEADER. WITH THE LEADER GONE, THEY WILL FIGHT AMONGST THEMSELVES.

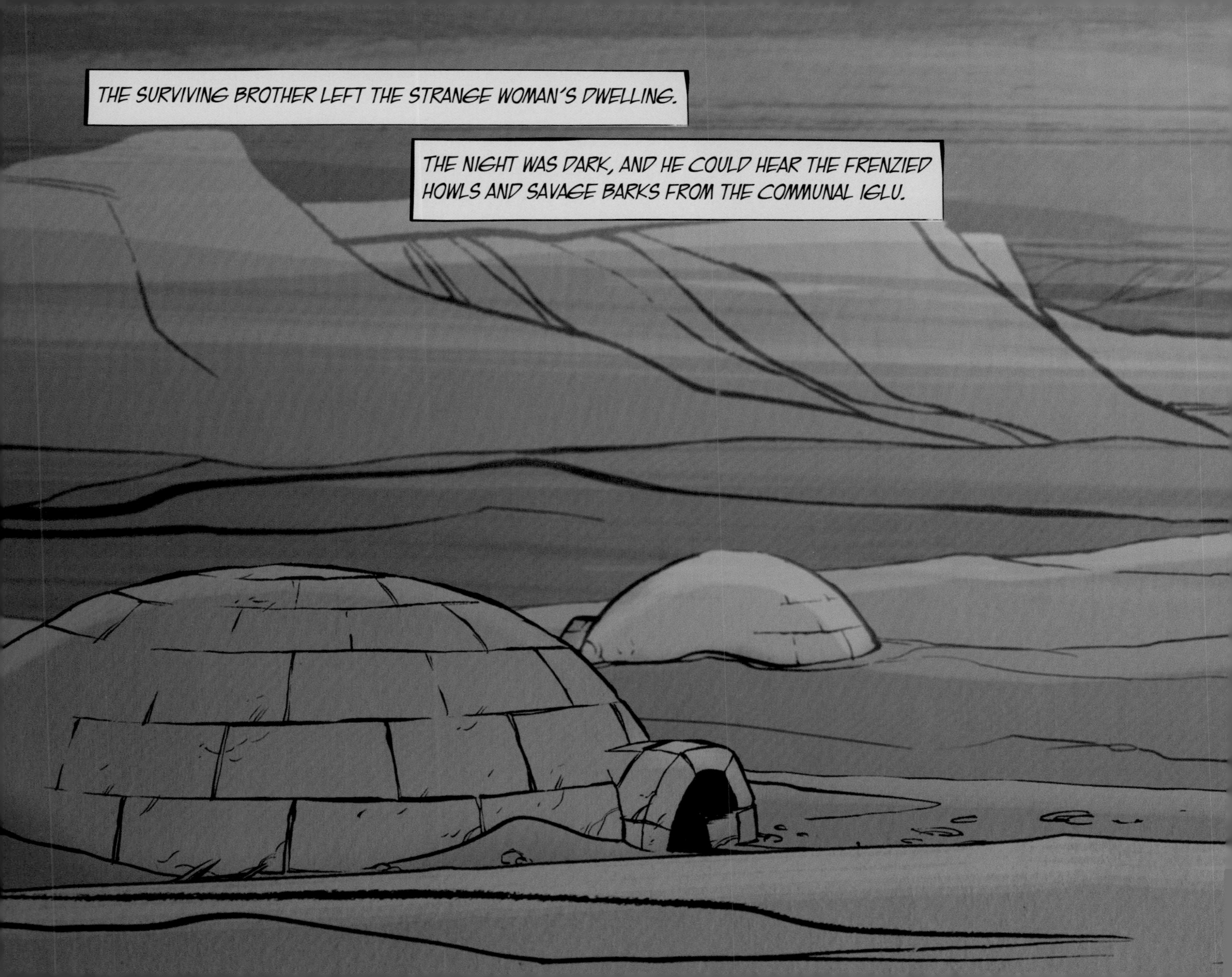
THE SURVIVING BROTHER LEFT THE STRANGE WOMAN'S DWELLING.
THE NIGHT WAS DARK, AND HE COULD HEAR THE FRENZIED HOWLS AND SAVAGE BARKS FROM THE COMMUNAL IGLU.

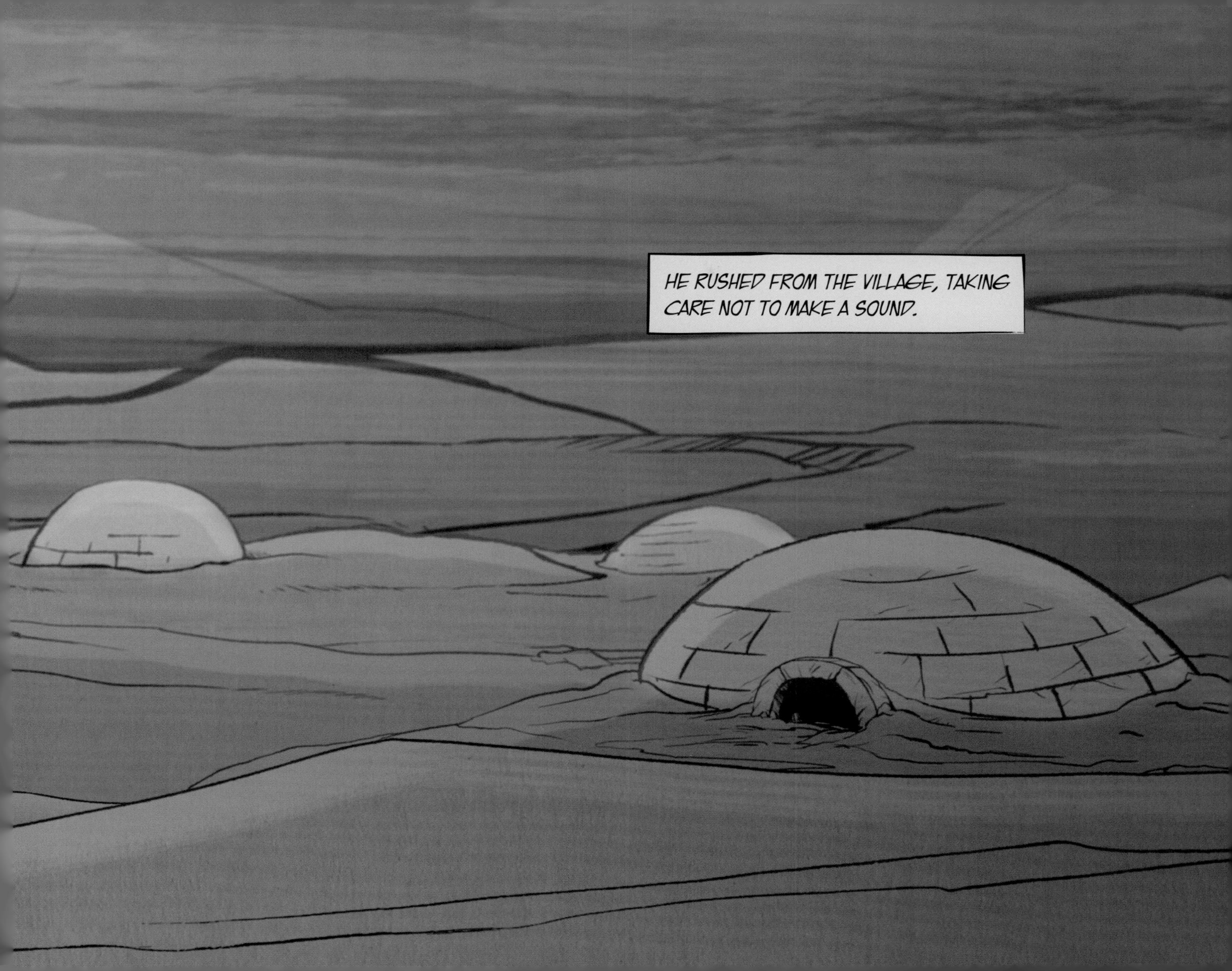
HE RUSHED FROM THE VILLAGE, TAKING CARE NOT TO MAKE A SOUND.

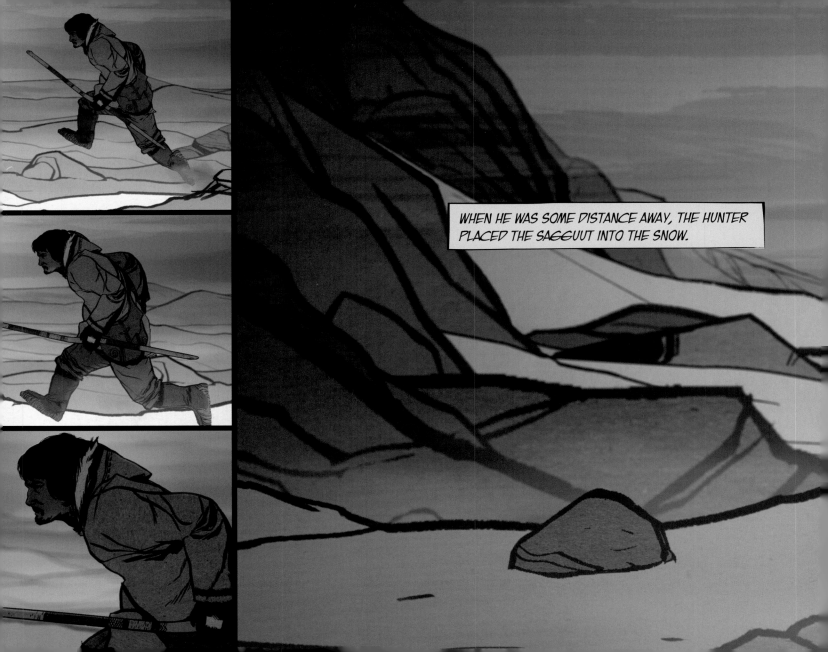

WHEN HE WAS SOME DISTANCE AWAY, THE HUNTER PLACED THE SAGGUUT INTO THE SNOW.

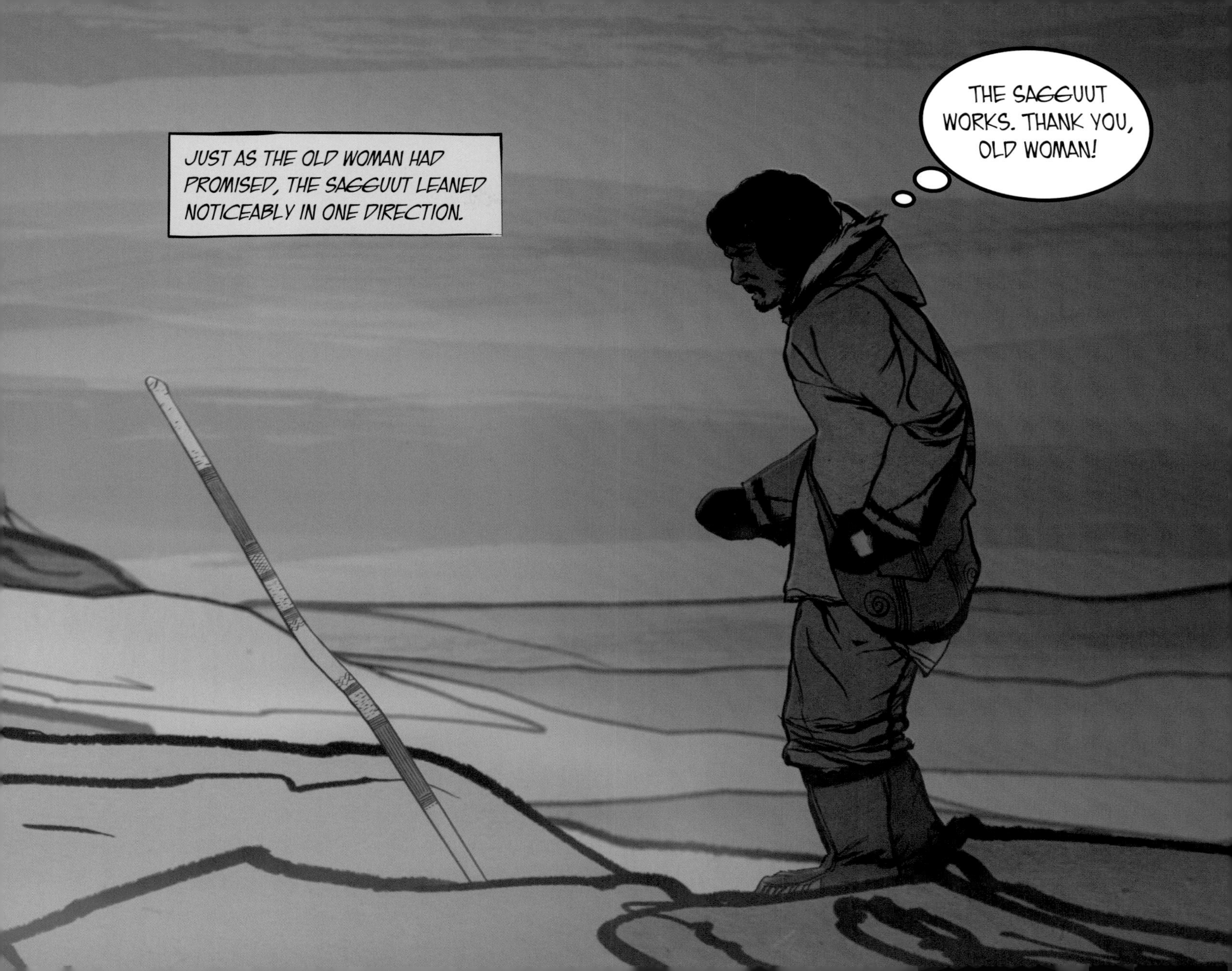
JUST AS THE OLD WOMAN HAD PROMISED, THE SAGGUUT LEANED NOTICEABLY IN ONE DIRECTION.
THE SAGGUUT WORKS. THANK YOU, OLD WOMAN!

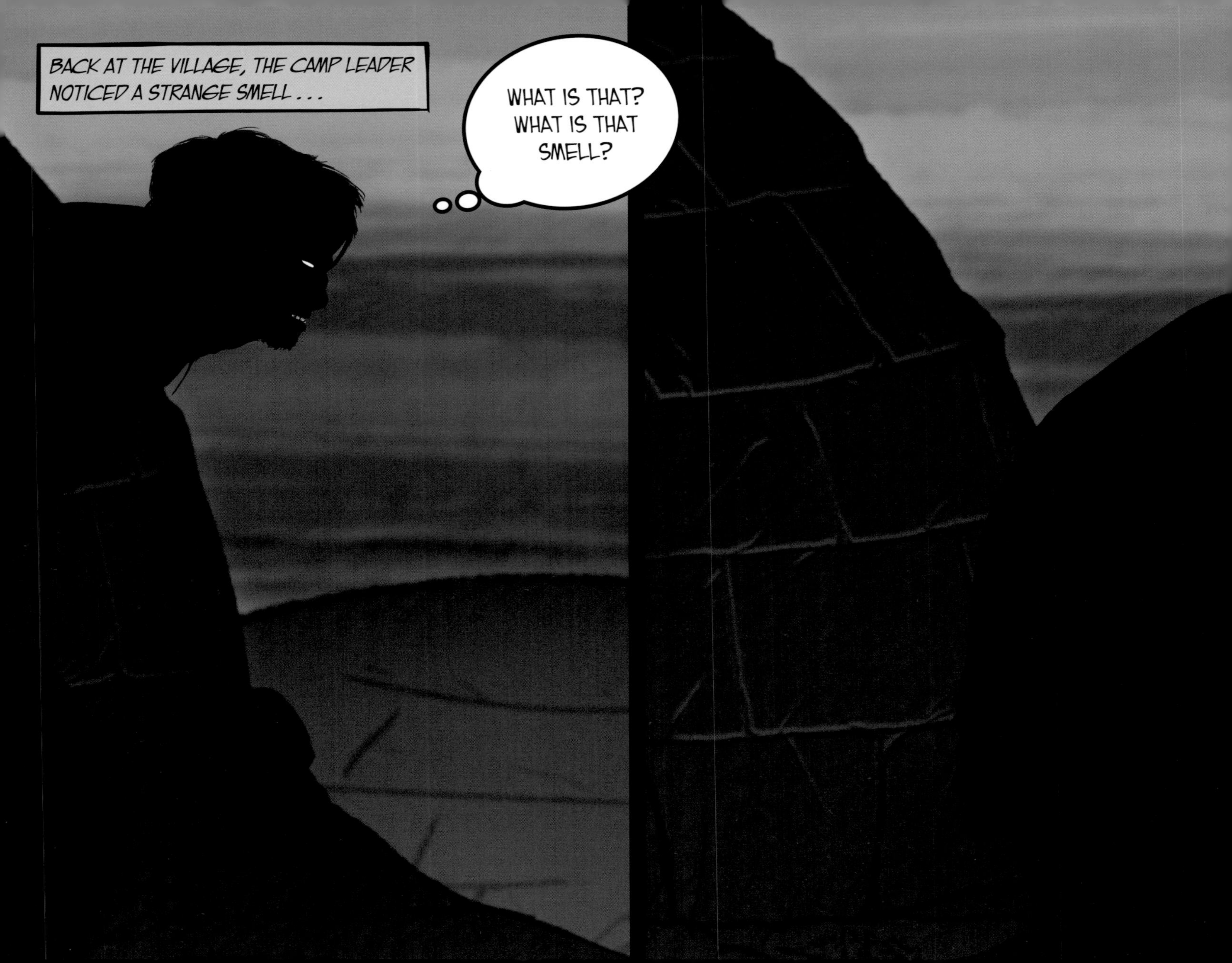
BACK AT THE VILLAGE, THE CAMP LEADER NOTICED A STRANGE SMELL . . .
WHAT IS THAT? WHAT IS THAT SMELL?

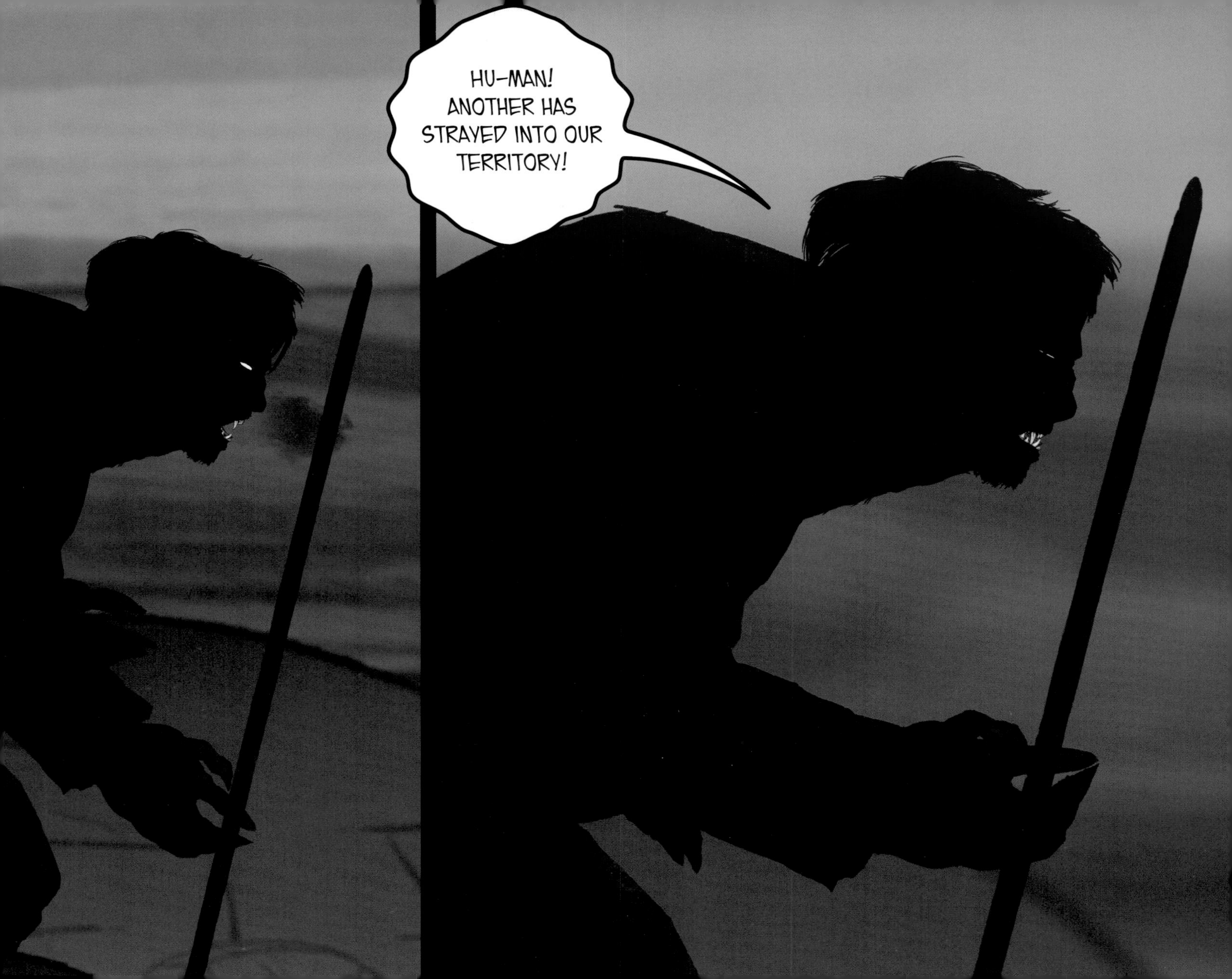
HU-MAN! ANOTHER HAS STRAYED INTO OUR TERRITORY!

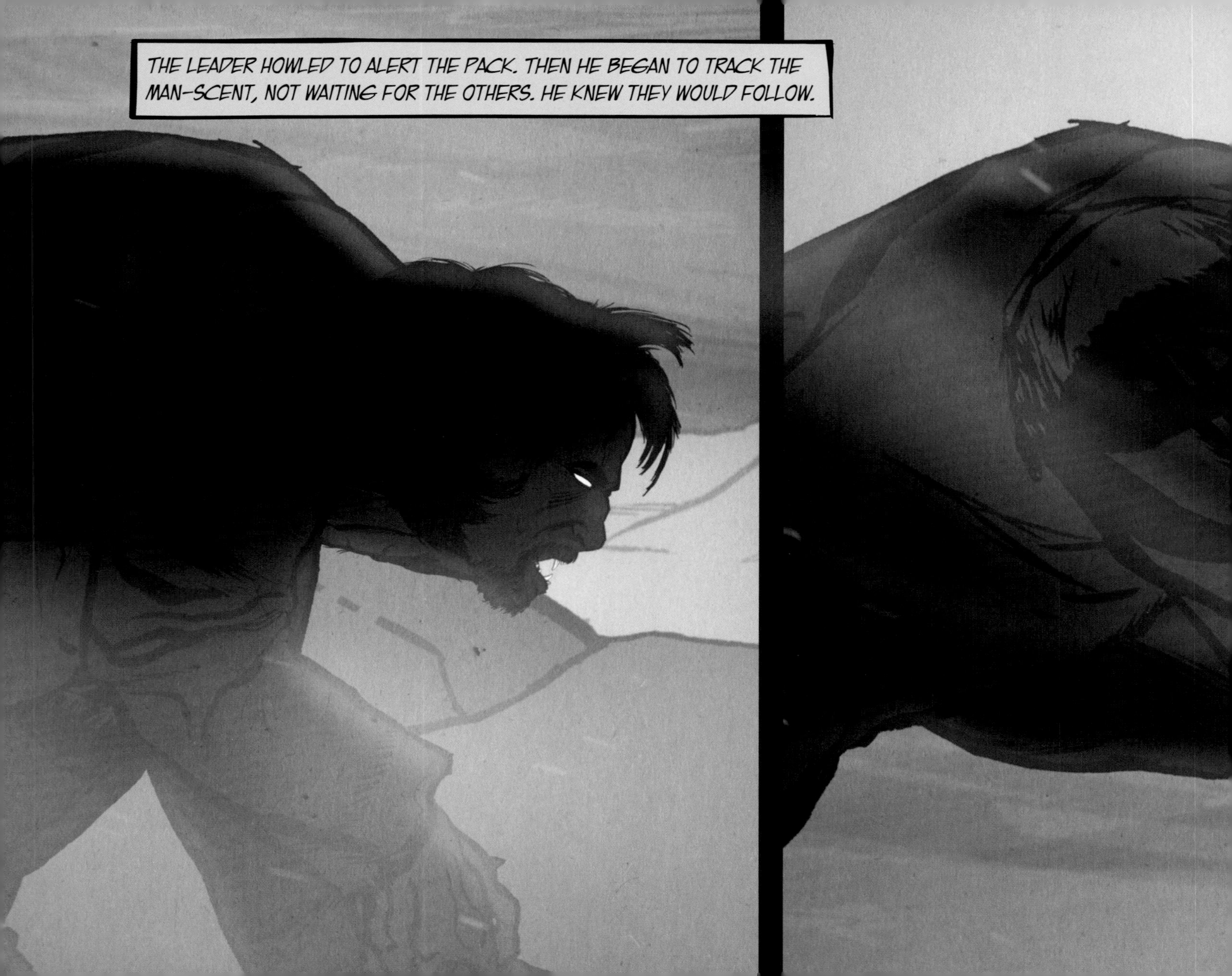
THE LEADER HOWLED TO ALERT THE PACK. THEN HE BEGAN TO TRACK THE MAN-SCENT, NOT WAITING FOR THE OTHERS. HE KNEW THEY WOULD FOLLOW.

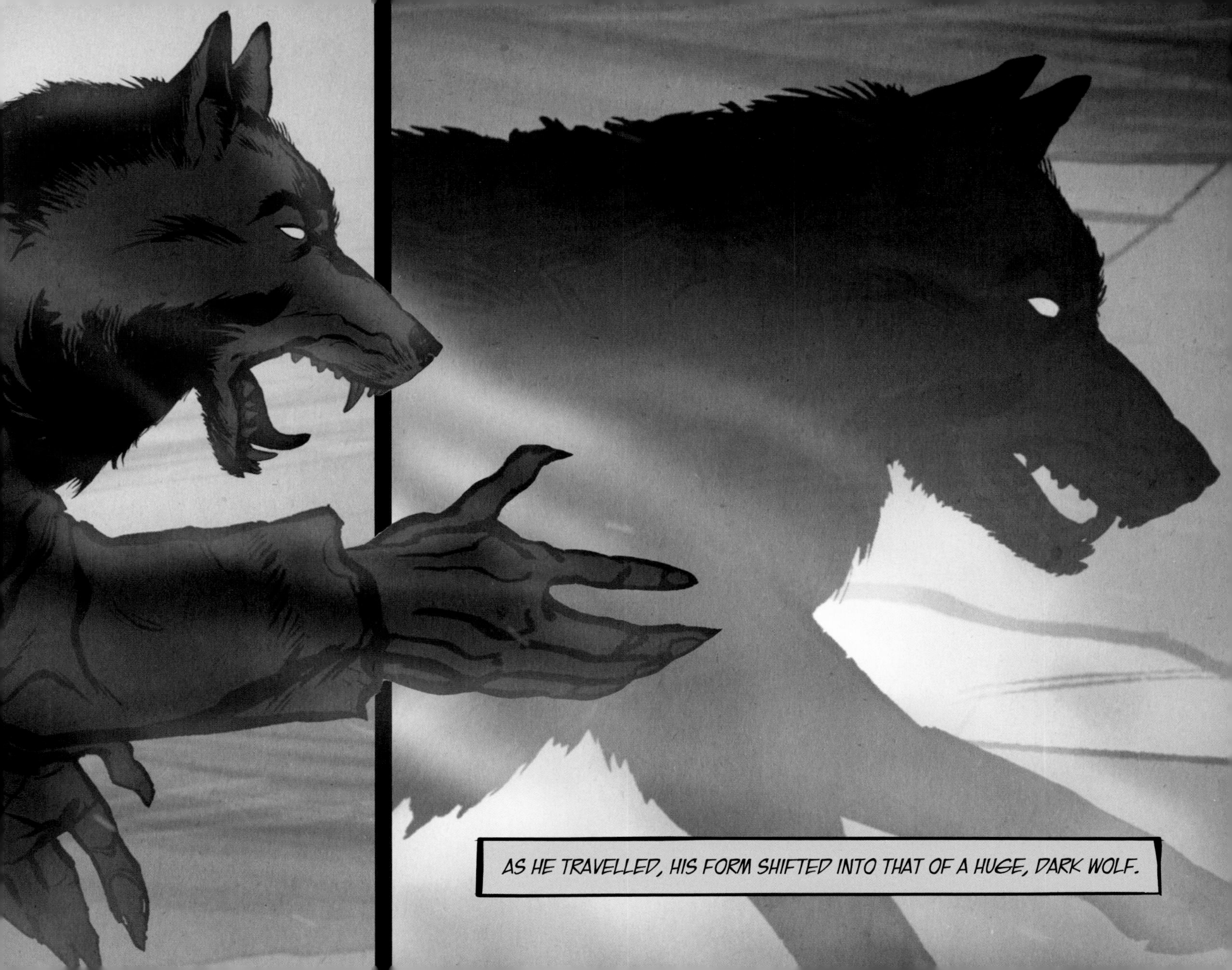
AS HE TRAVELLED, HIS FORM SHIFTED INTO THAT OF A HUGE, DARK WOLF.

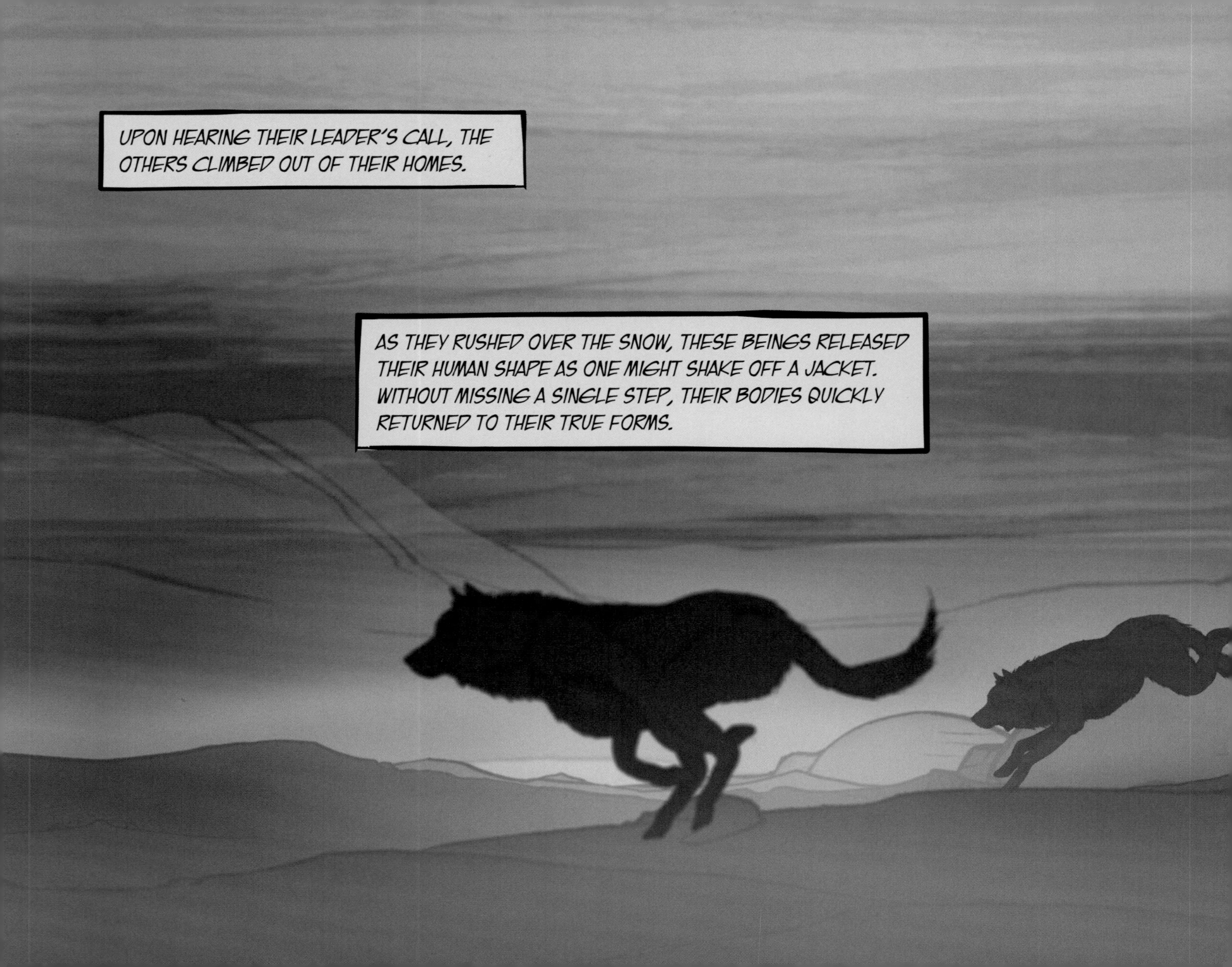
UPON HEARING THEIR LEADER'S CALL, THE OTHERS CLIMBED OUT OF THEIR HOMES.
AS THEY RUSHED OVER THE SNOW, THESE BEINGS RELEASED THEIR HUMAN SHAPE AS ONE MIGHT SHAKE OFF A JACKET. WITHOUT MISSING A SINGLE STEP, THEIR BODIES QUICKLY RETURNED TO THEIR TRUE FORMS.

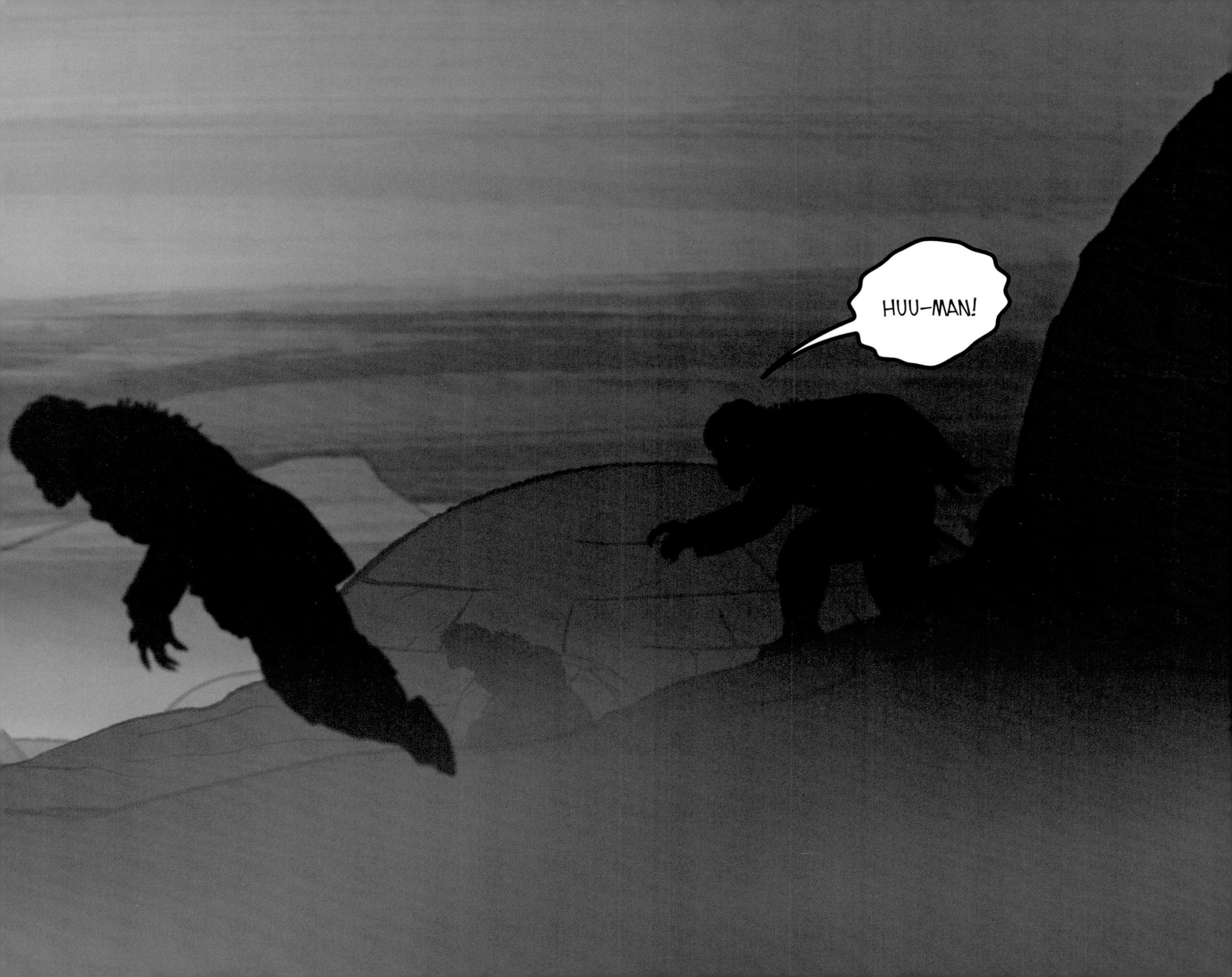
HUU-MAN!

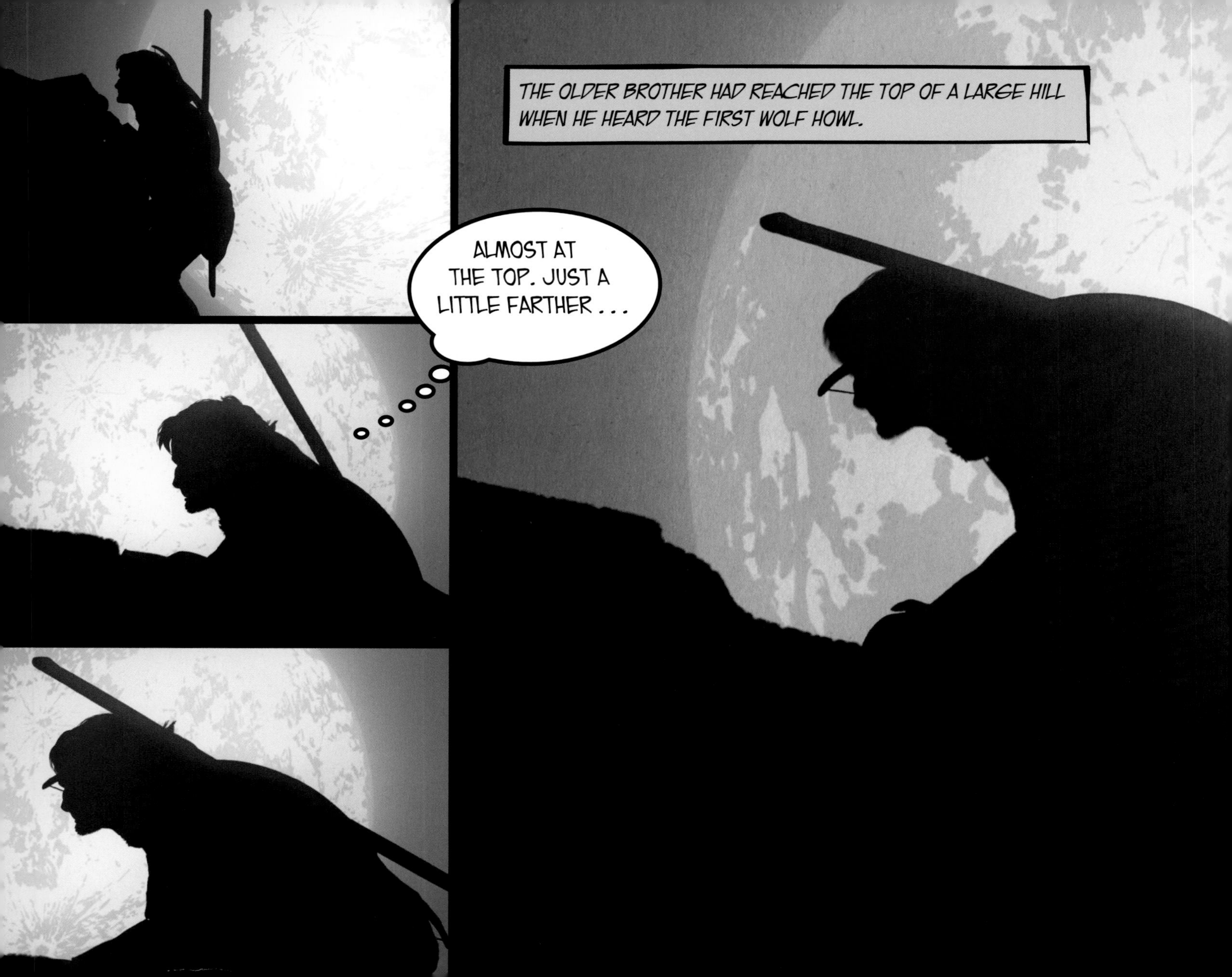
THE OLDER BROTHER HAD REACHED THE TOP OF A LARGE HILL WHEN HE HEARD THE FIRST WOLF HOWL.
ALMOST AT THE TOP. JUST A LITTLE FARTHER . . .

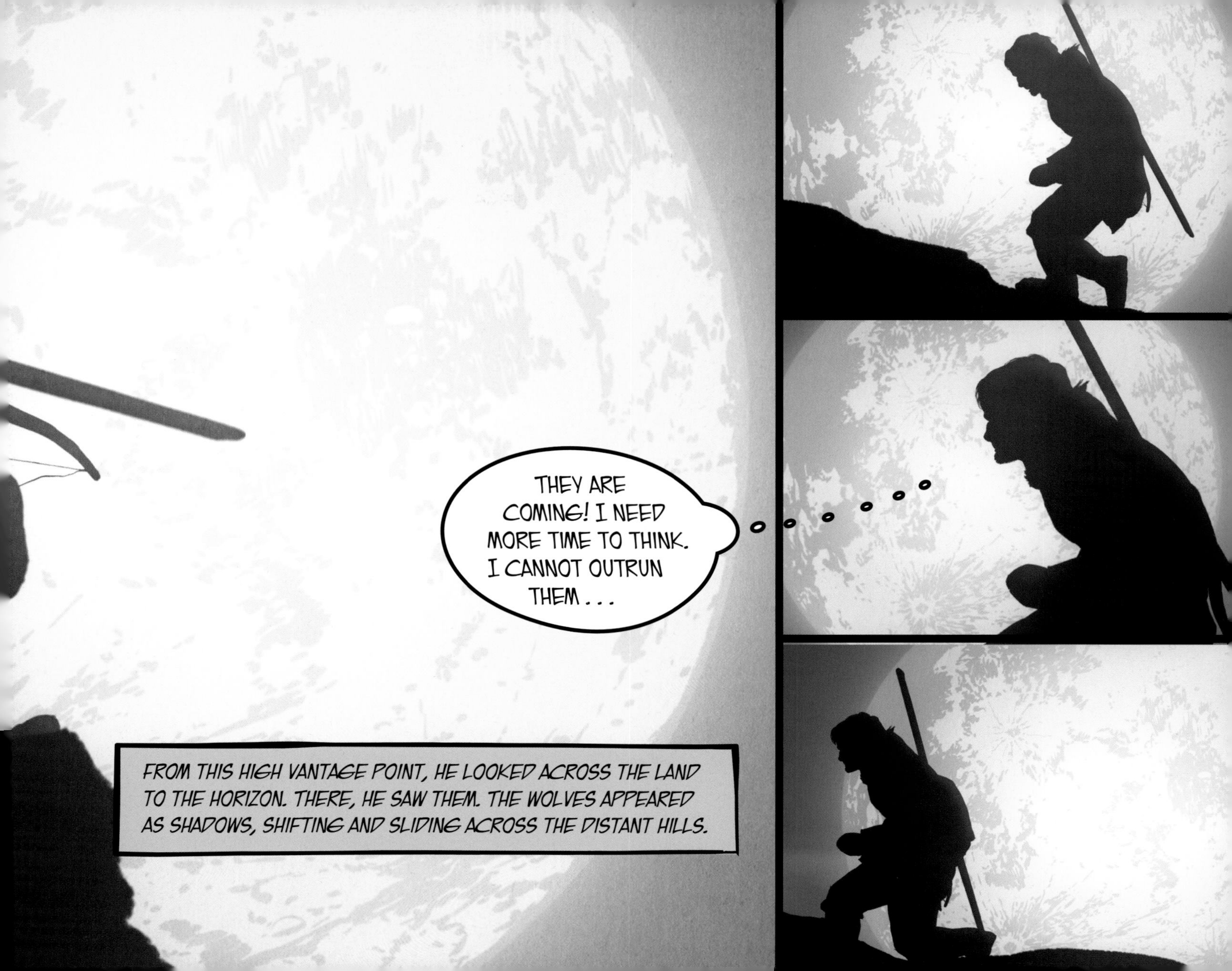
THEY ARE COMING! I NEED MORE TIME TO THINK. I CANNOT OUTRUN THEM . . .
FROM THIS HIGH VANTAGE POINT, HE LOOKED ACROSS THE LAND TO THE HORIZON. THERE, HE SAW THEM. THE WOLVES APPEARED AS SHADOWS, SHIFTING AND SLIDING ACROSS THE DISTANT HILLS.

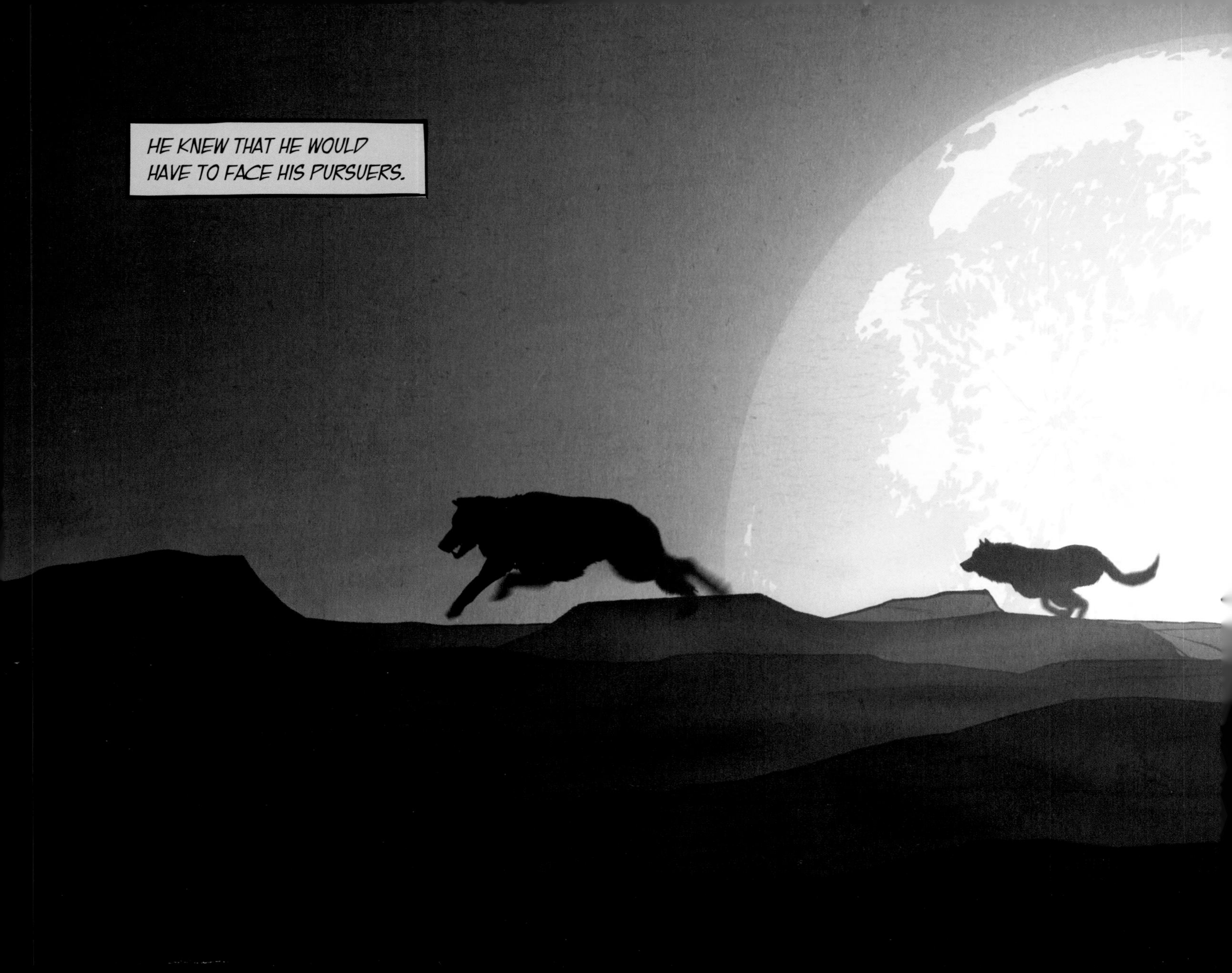
HE KNEW THAT HE WOULD HAVE TO FACE HIS PURSUERS.

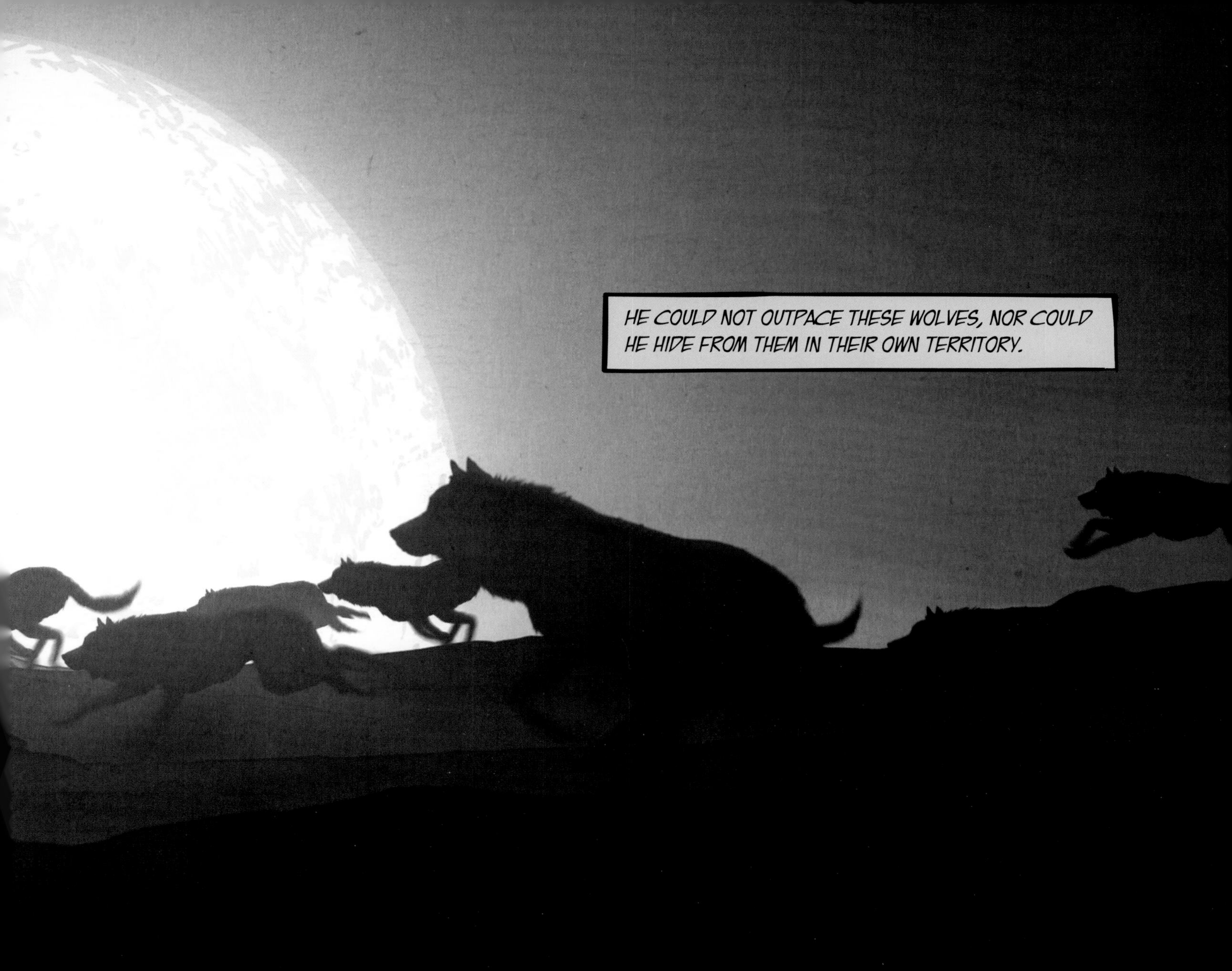
HE COULD NOT OUTPACE THESE WOLVES, NOR COULD HE HIDE FROM THEM IN THEIR OWN TERRITORY.

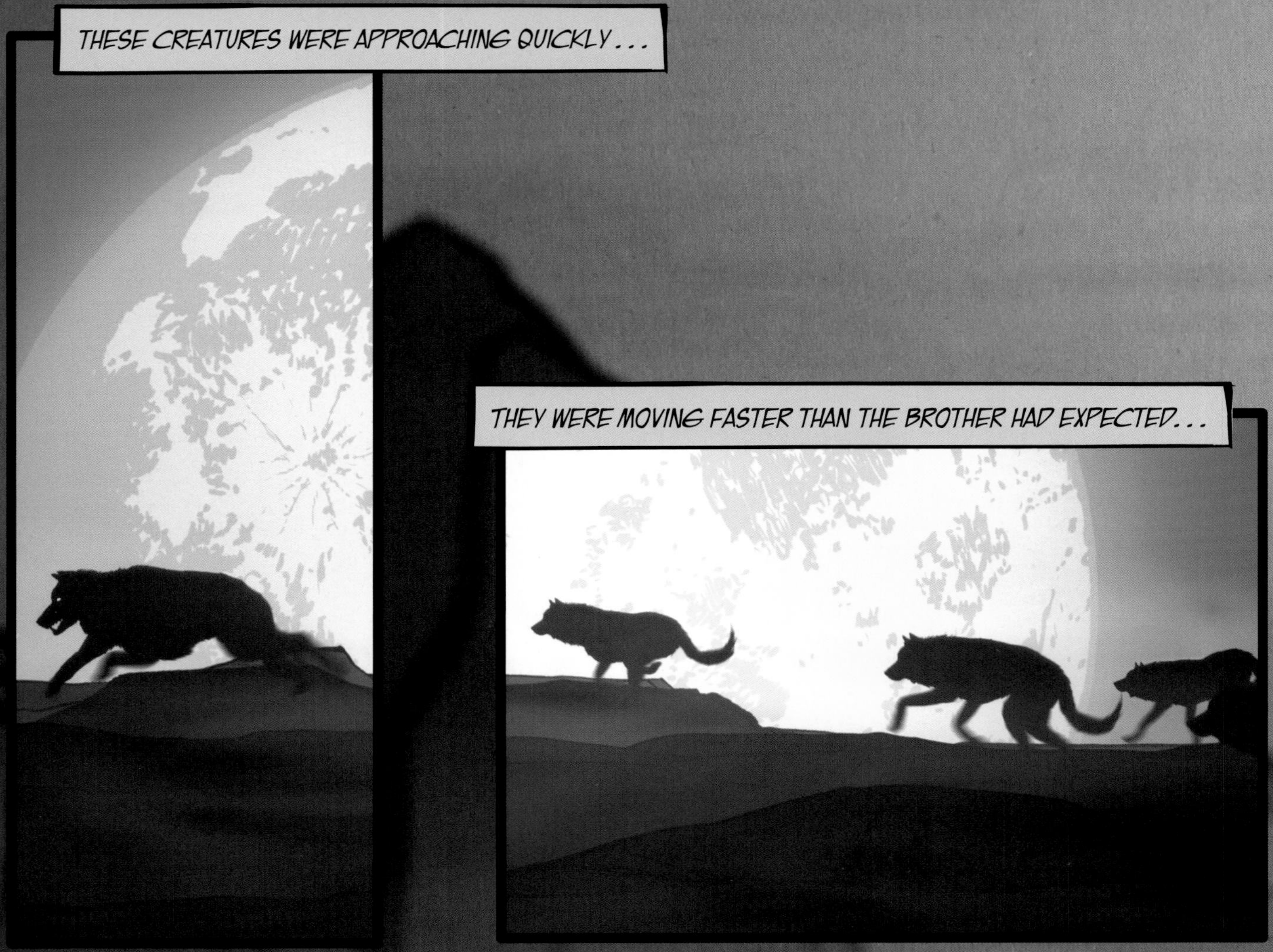
THESE CREATURES WERE APPROACHING QUICKLY . . .
THEY WERE MOVING FASTER THAN THE BROTHER HAD EXPECTED . . .

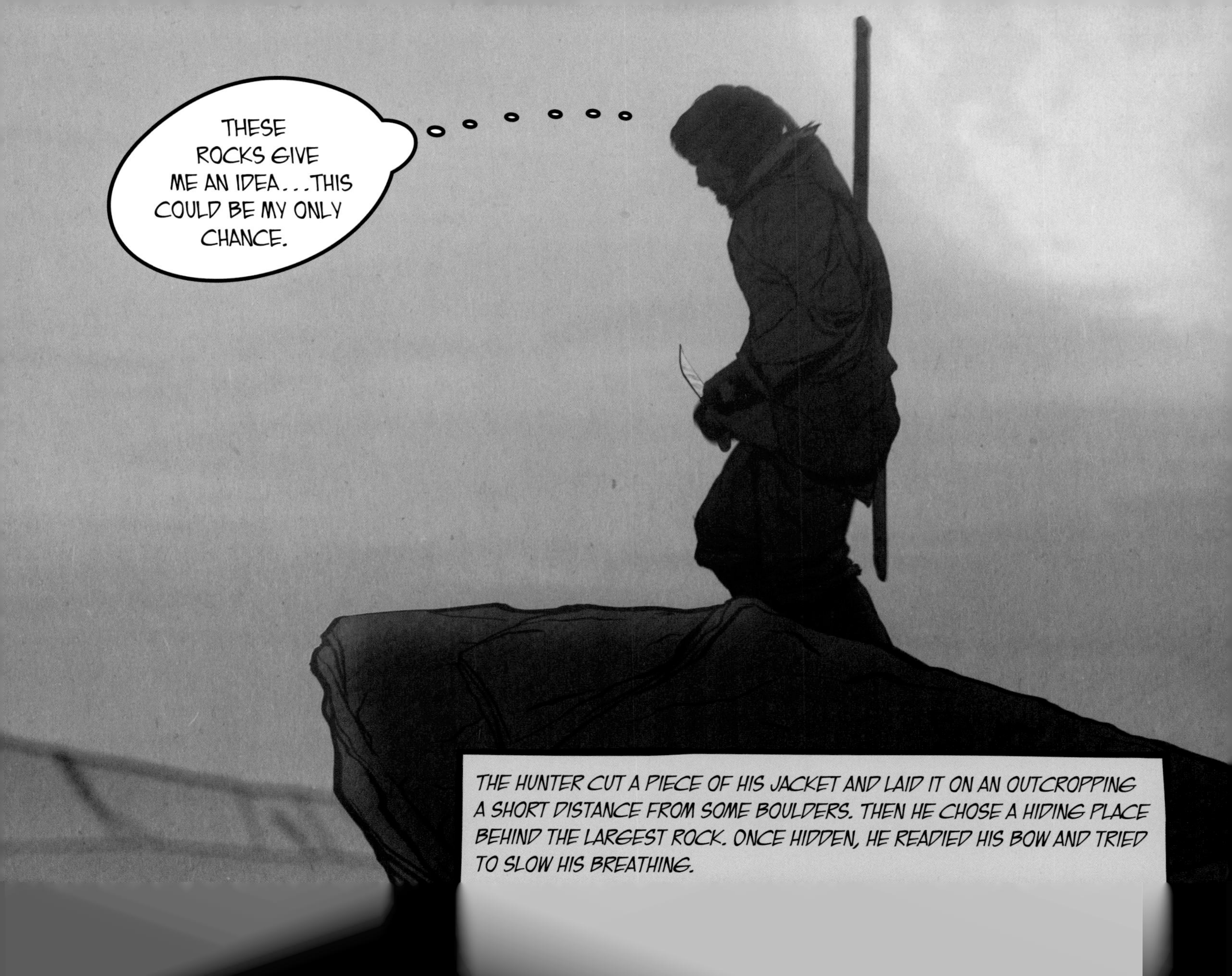
THESE ROCKS GIVE ME AN IDEA . . . THIS COULD BE MY ONLY CHANCE.
THE HUNTER CUT A PIECE OF HIS JACKET AND LAID IT ON AN OUTCROPPING A SHORT DISTANCE FROM SOME BOULDERS. THEN HE CHOSE A HIDING PLACE BEHIND THE LARGEST ROCK. ONCE HIDDEN, HE READIED HIS BOW AND TRIED TO SLOW HIS BREATHING.

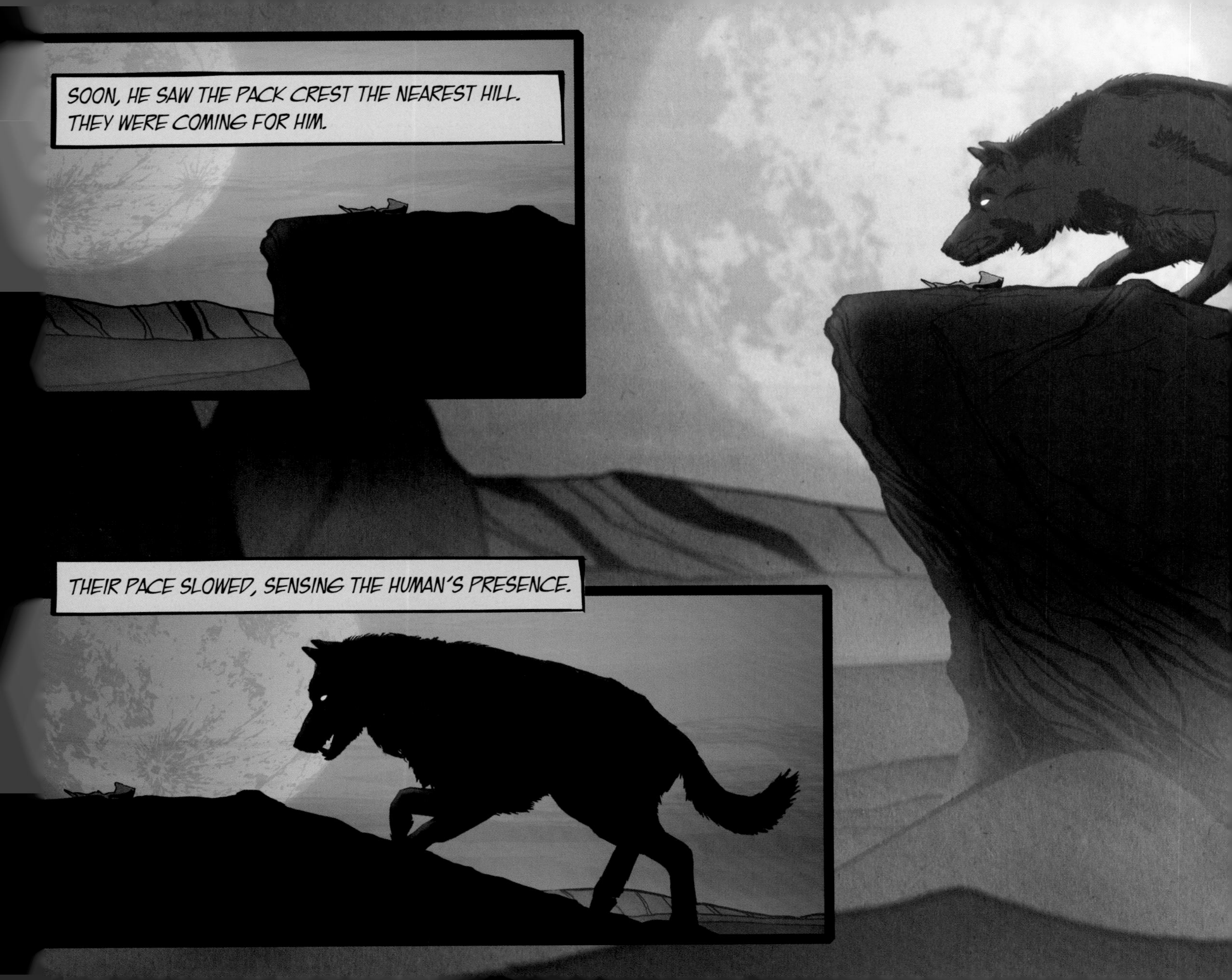
SOON, HE SAW THE PACK CREST THE NEAREST HILL. THEY WERE COMING FOR HIM.
THEIR PACE SLOWED, SENSING THE HUMAN'S PRESENCE.

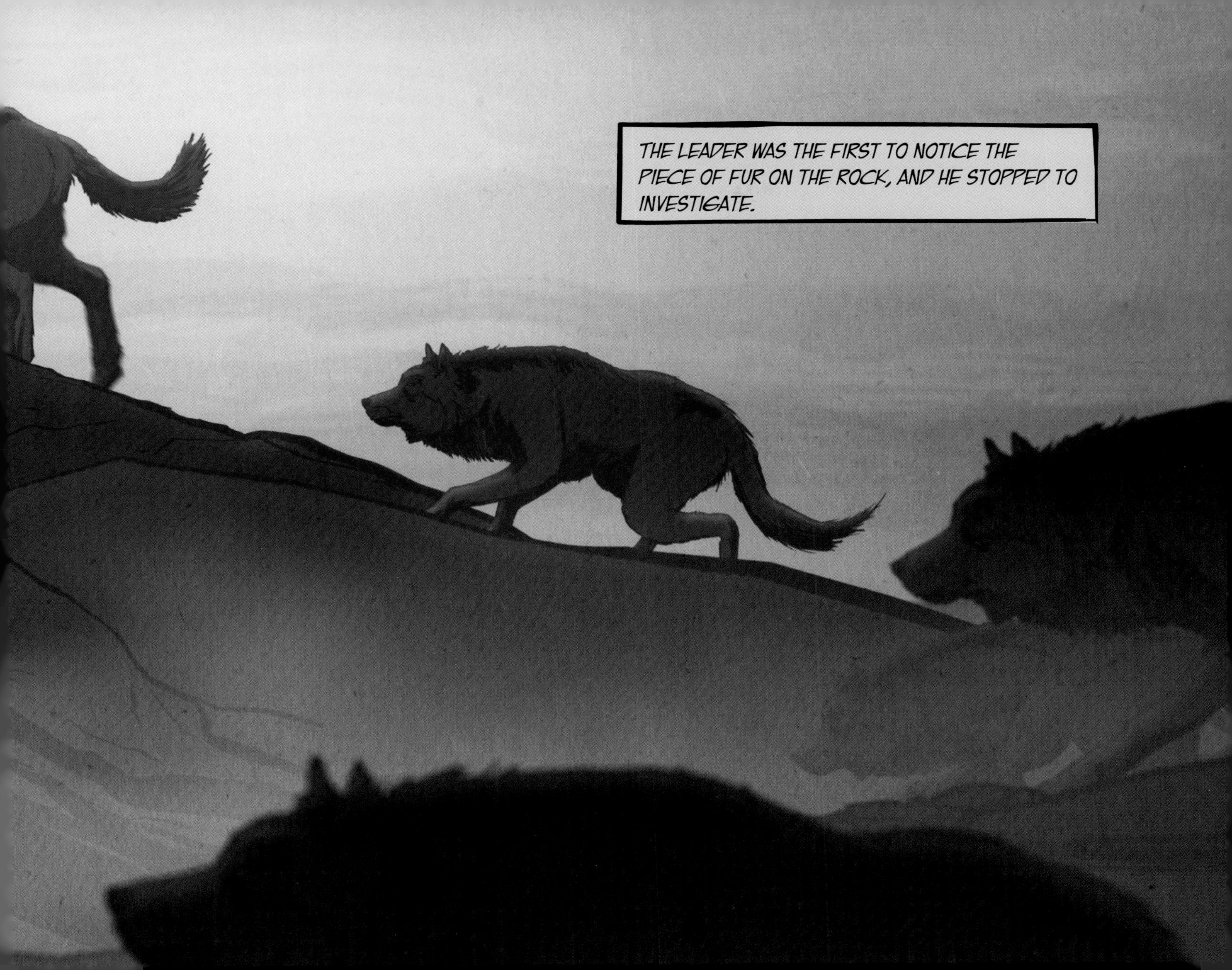
THE LEADER WAS THE FIRST TO NOTICE THE PIECE OF FUR ON THE ROCK, AND HE STOPPED TO INVESTIGATE.

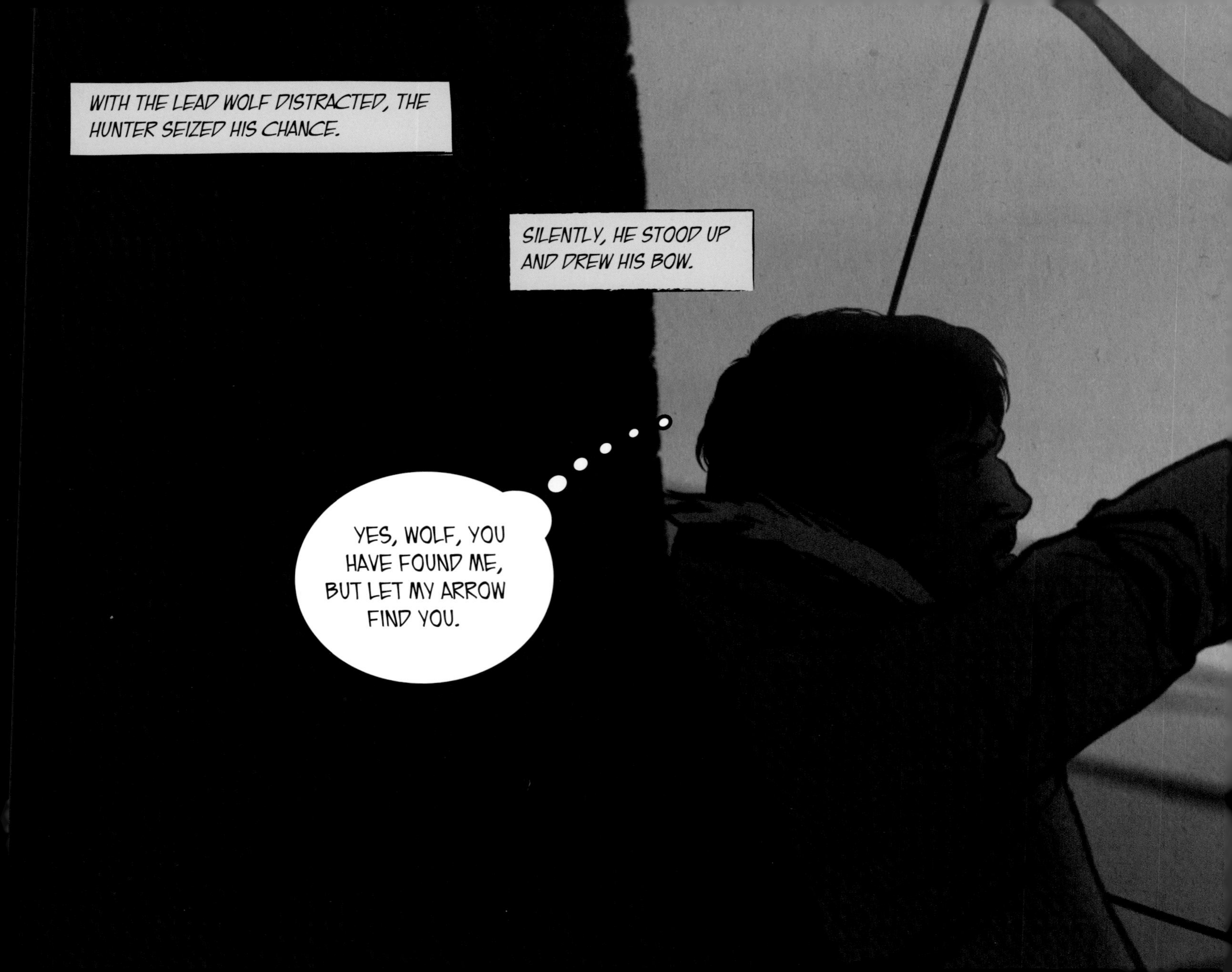
WITH THE LEAD WOLF DISTRACTED, THE HUNTER SEIZED HIS CHANCE.
SILENTLY, HE STOOD UP AND DREW HIS BOW.
YES, WOLF, YOU HAVE FOUND ME, BUT LET MY ARROW FIND YOU.

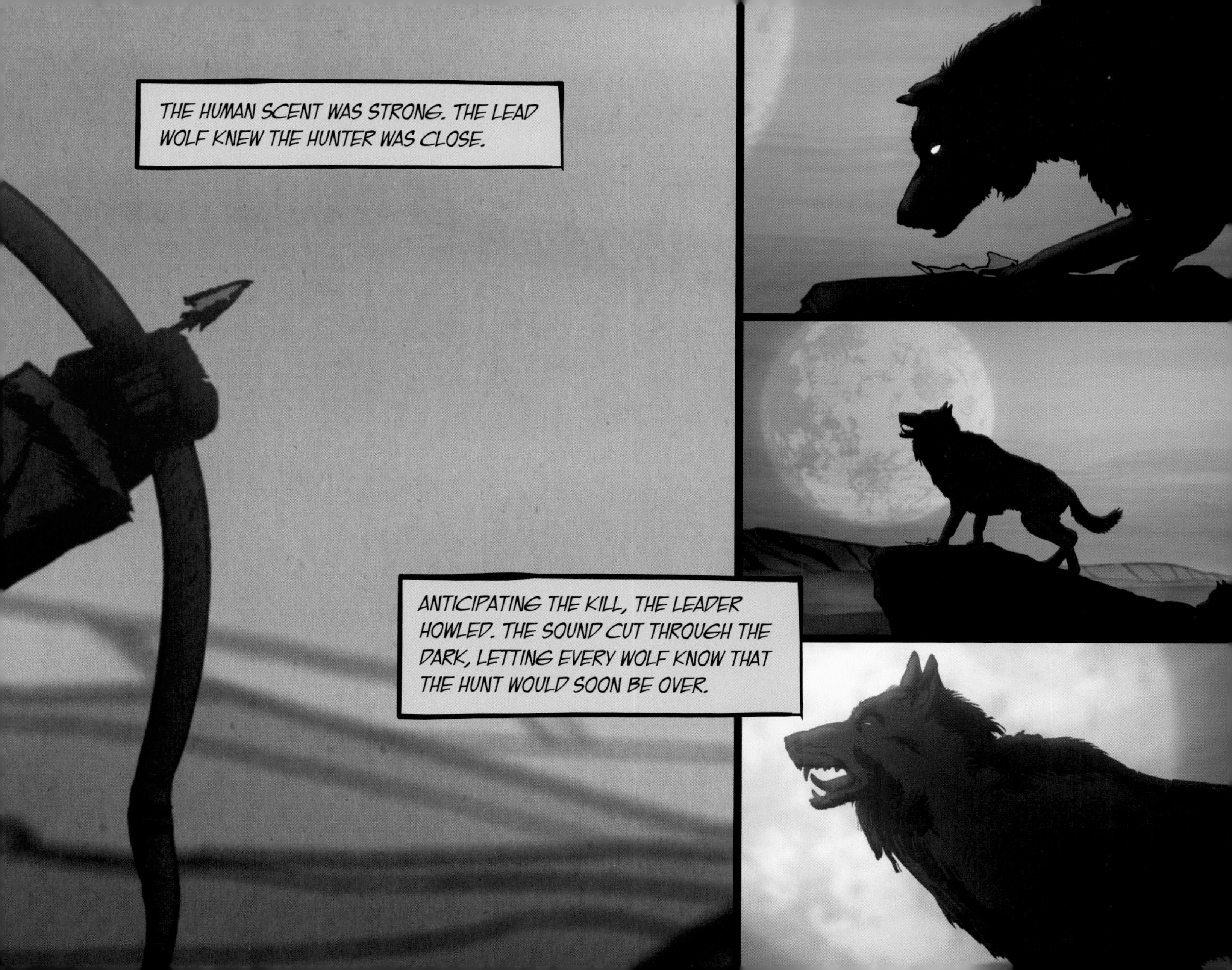
THE HUMAN SCENT WAS STRONG. THE LEAD WOLF KNEW THE HUNTER WAS CLOSE.
ANTICIPATING THE KILL, THE LEADER HOWLED. THE SOUND CUT THROUGH THE DARK, LETTING EVERY WOLF KNOW THAT THE HUNT WOULD SOON BE OVER.

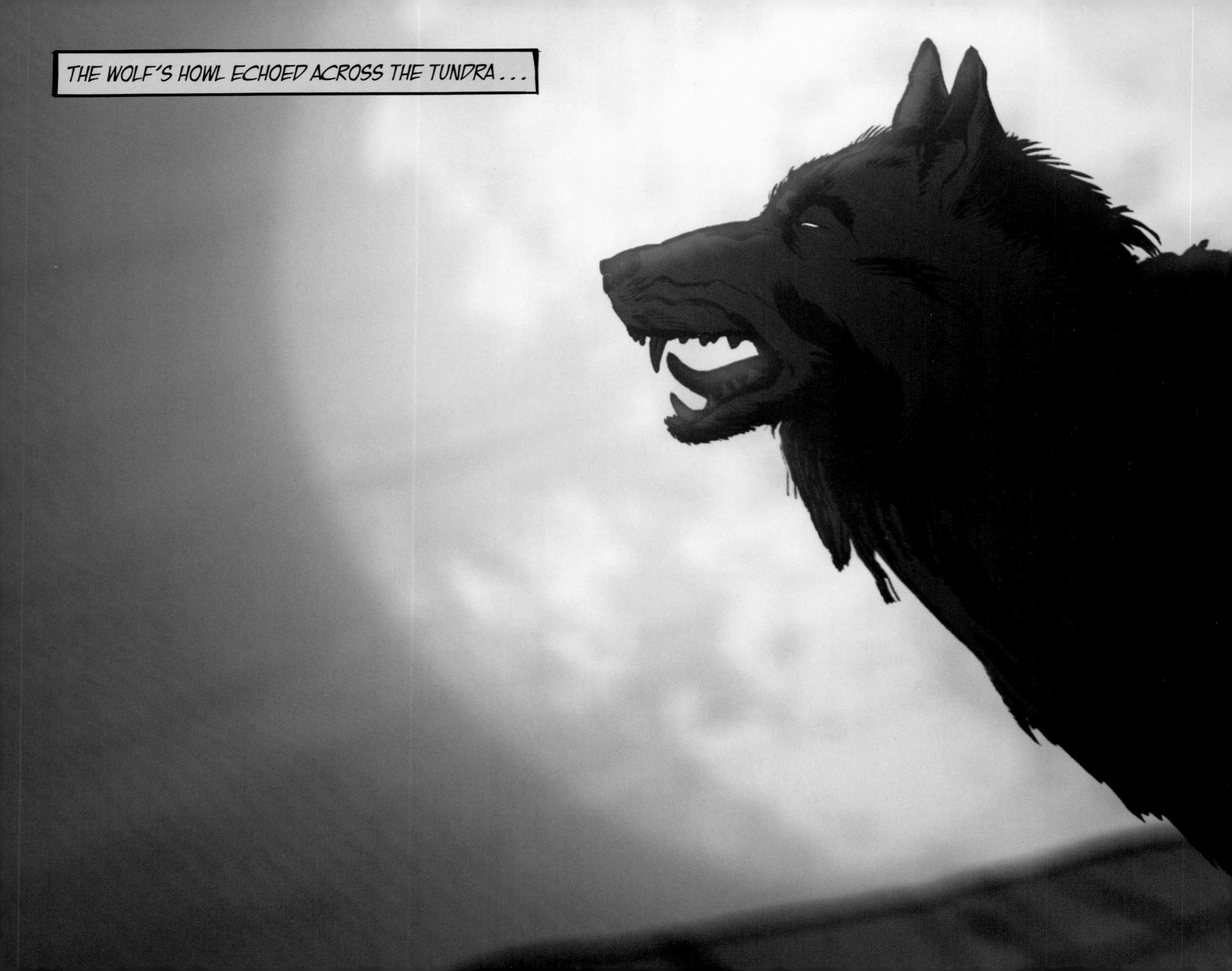
THE WOLF'S HOWL ECHOED ACROSS THE TUNDRA . . .

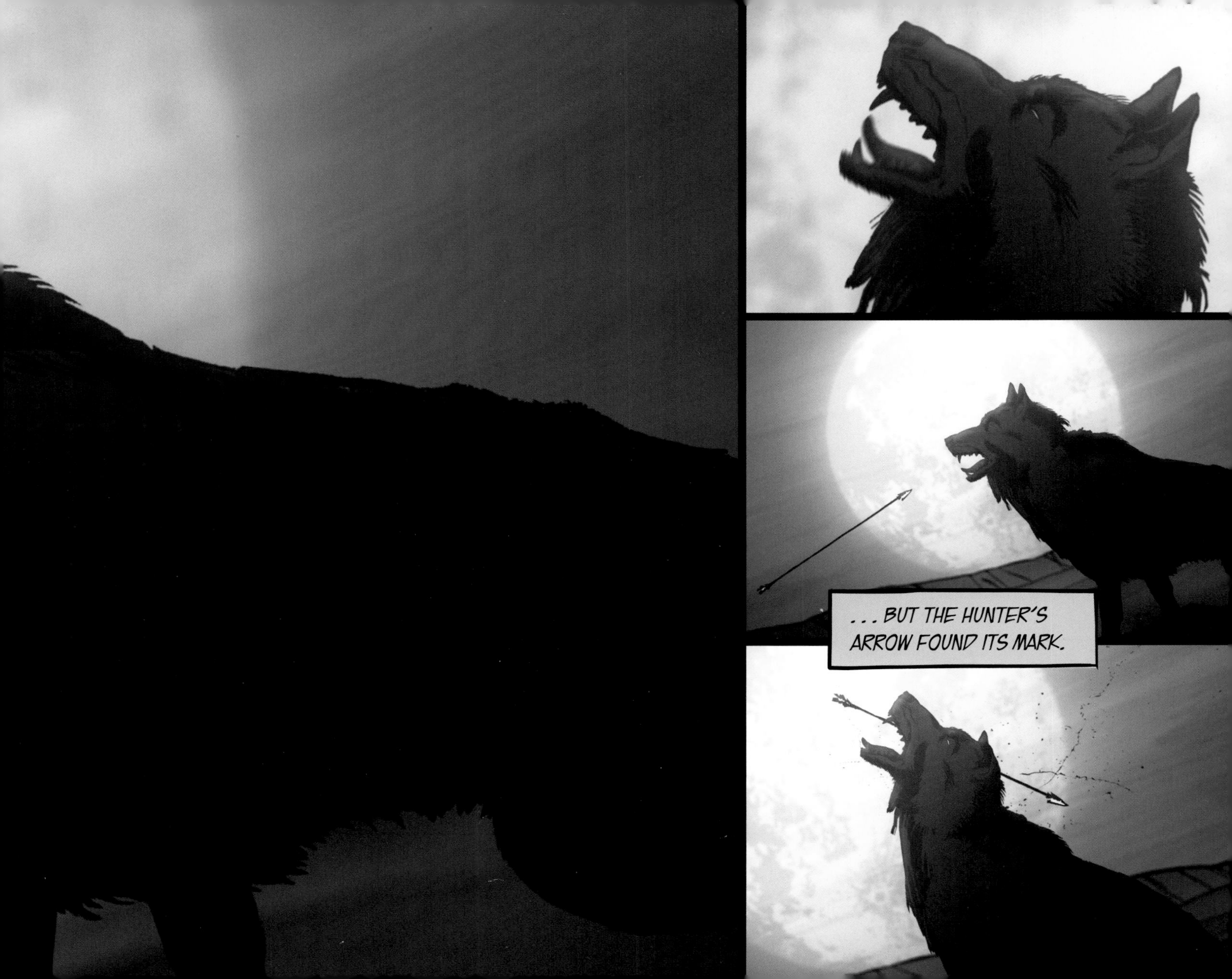
. . . BUT THE HUNTER'S ARROW FOUND ITS MARK.

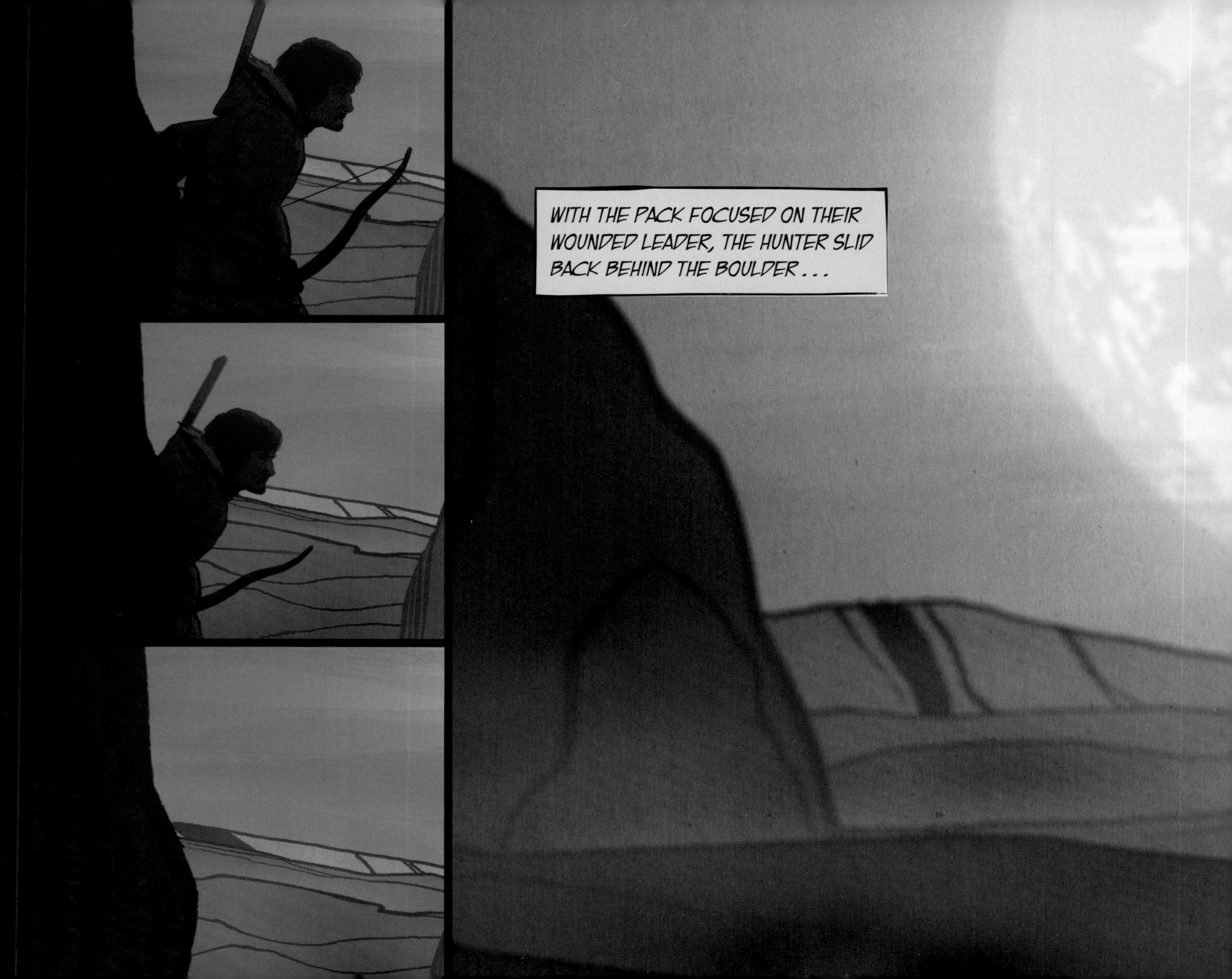
WITH THE PACK FOCUSED ON THEIR WOUNDED LEADER, THE HUNTER SLID BACK BEHIND THE BOULDER . . .

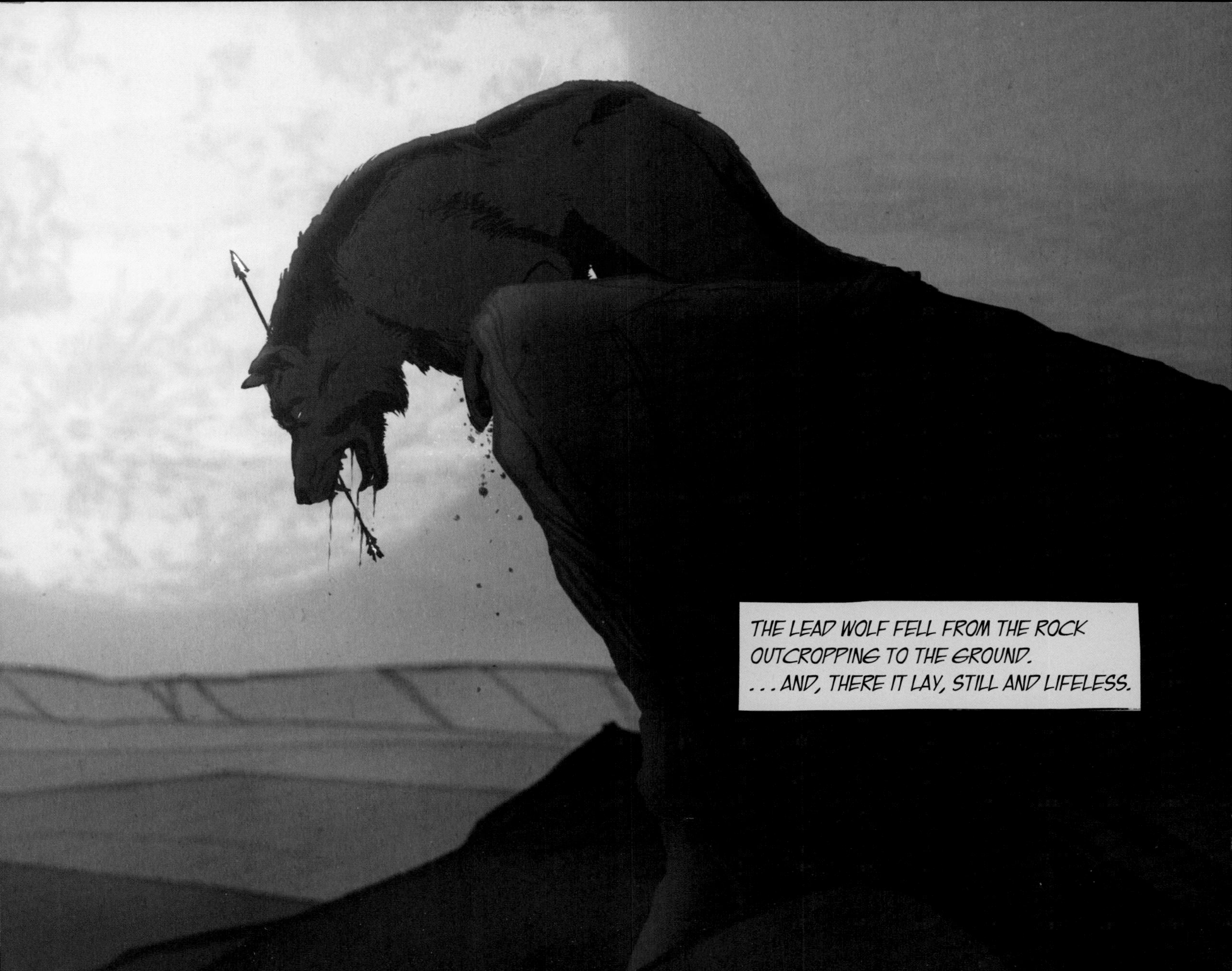
THE LEAD WOLF FELL FROM THE ROCK OUTCROPPING TO THE GROUND.
. . . AND, THERE IT LAY, STILL AND LIFELESS.

THE OLD WOMAN'S WORDS PROVED TRUE.
THE WOLVES ABANDONED ANY THOUGHT OF THE HUNT AND POUNCED ON THEIR FALLEN LEADER . . .

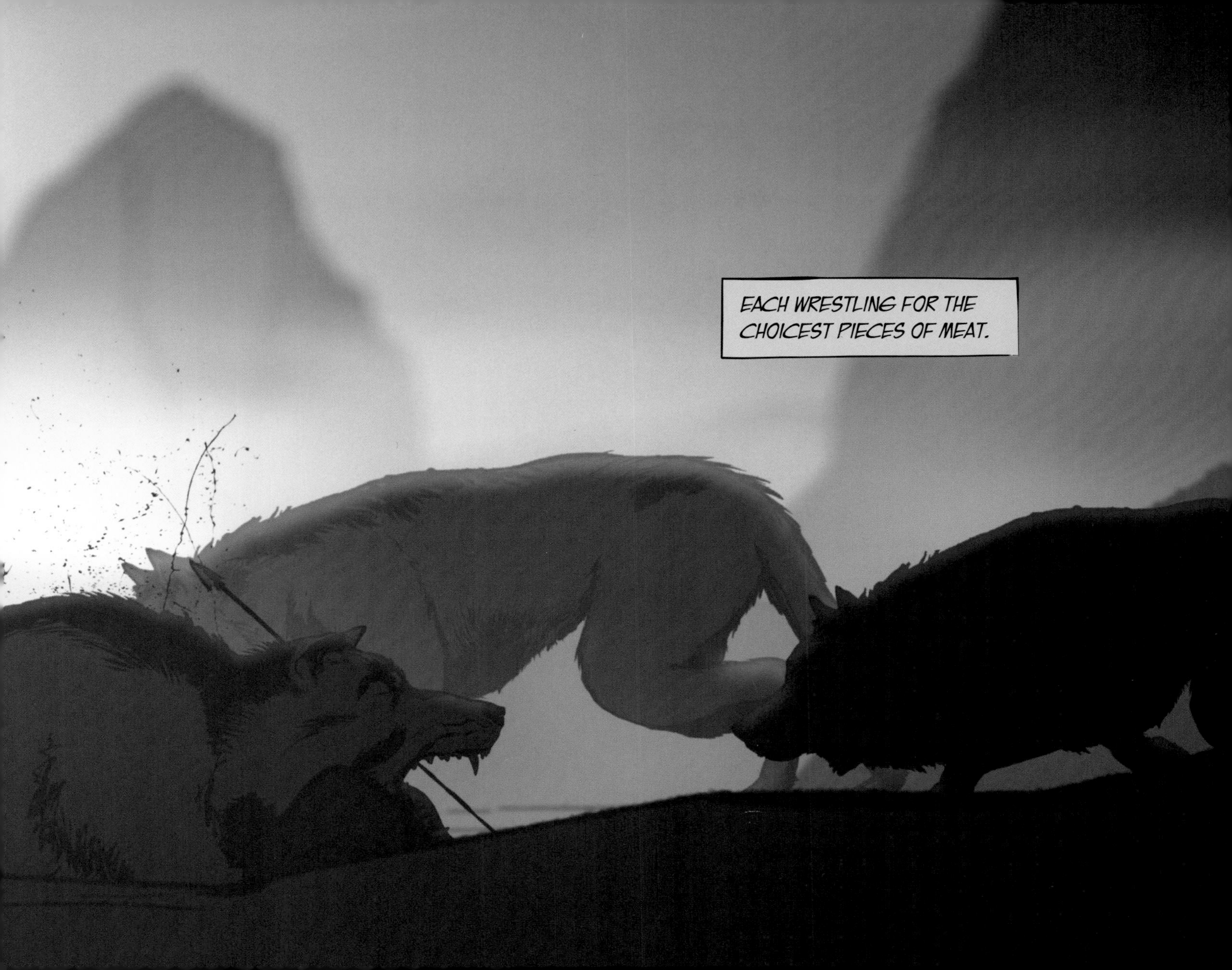
EACH WRESTLING FOR THE CHOICEST PIECES OF MEAT.

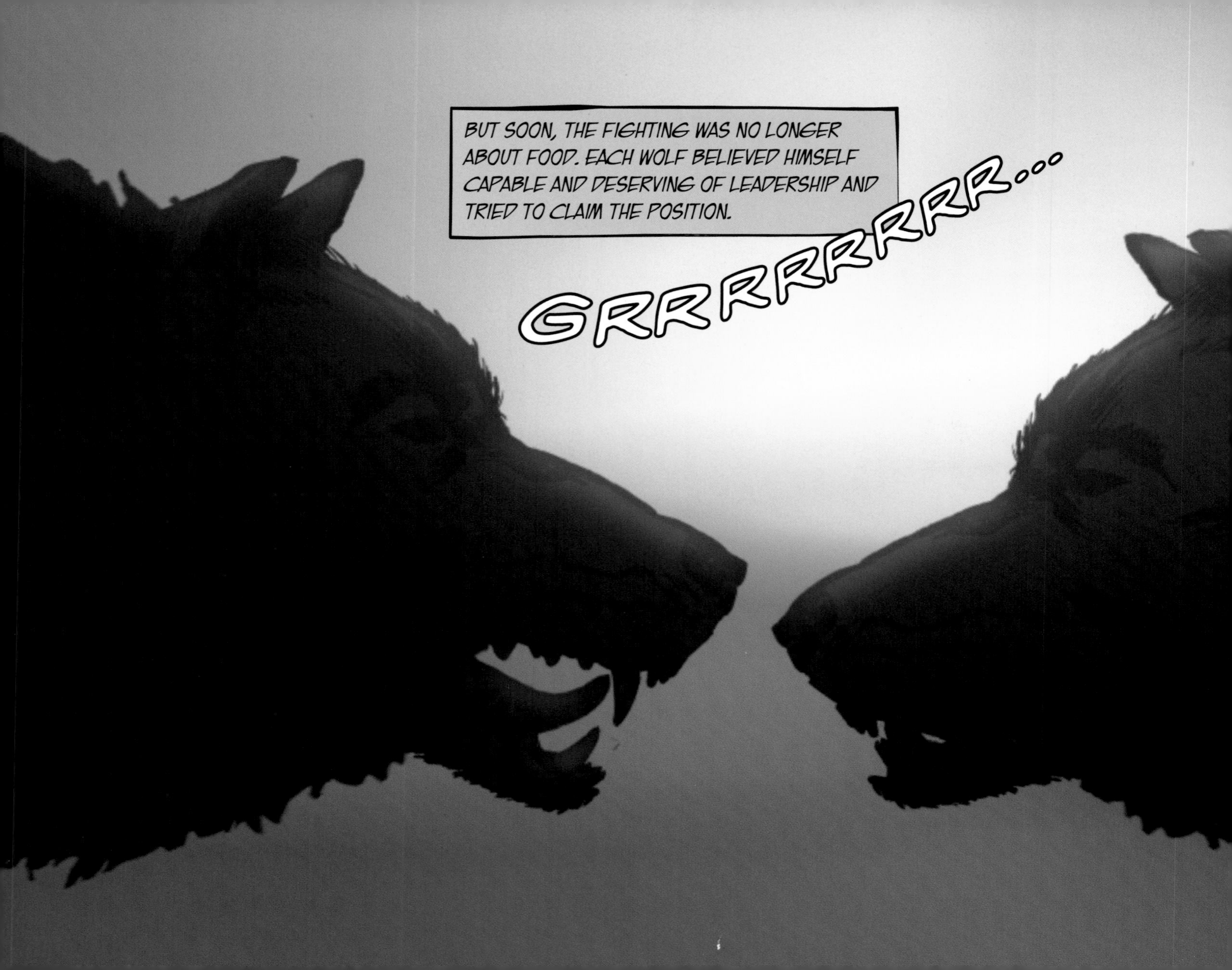
BUT SOON, THE FIGHTING WAS NO LONGER ABOUT FOOD. EACH WOLF BELIEVED HIMSELF CAPABLE AND DESERVING OF LEADERSHIP AND TRIED TO CLAIM THE POSITION.
GRRRRRRRRR...

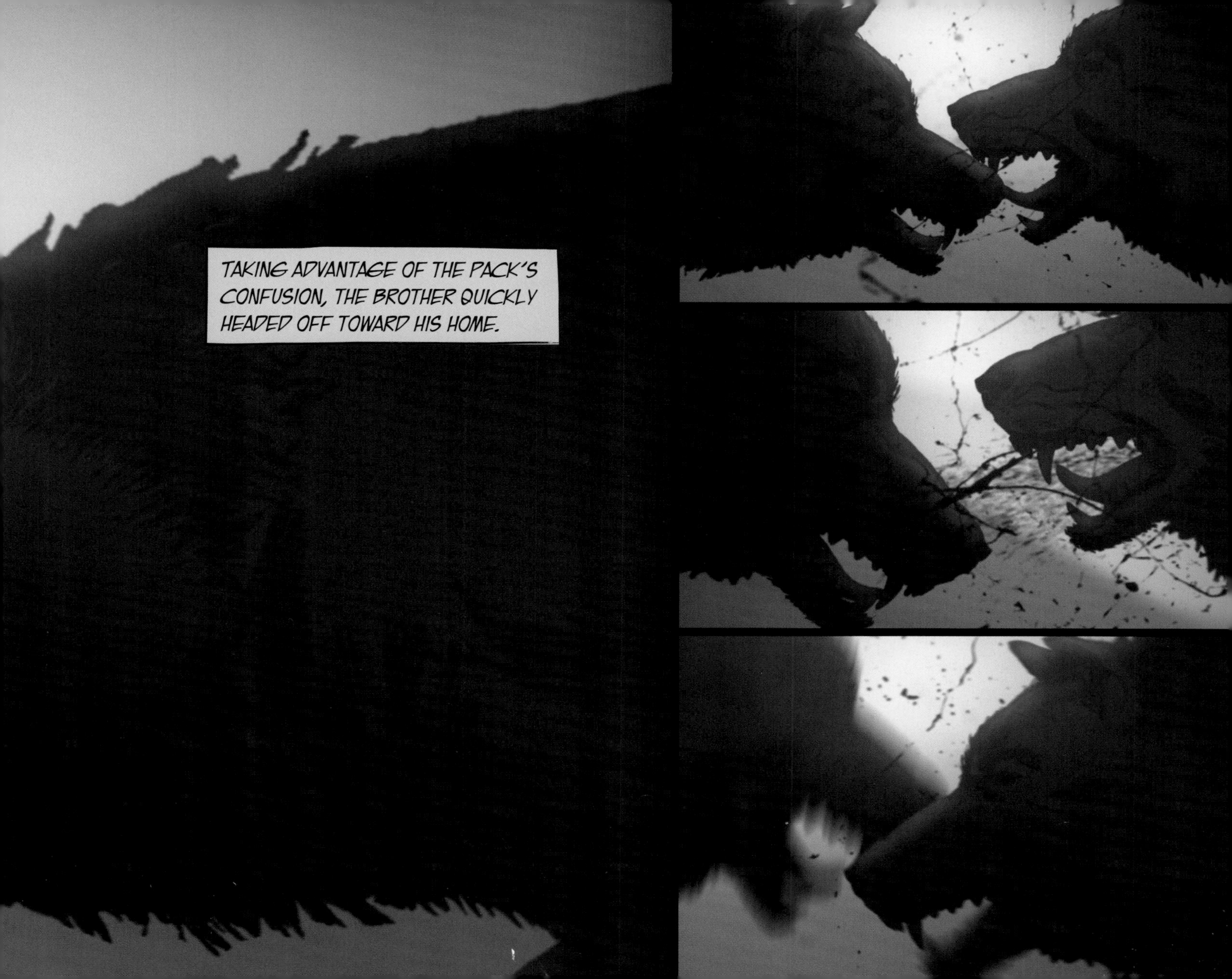
TAKING ADVANTAGE OF THE PACK'S CONFUSION, THE BROTHER QUICKLY HEADED OFF TOWARD HIS HOME.

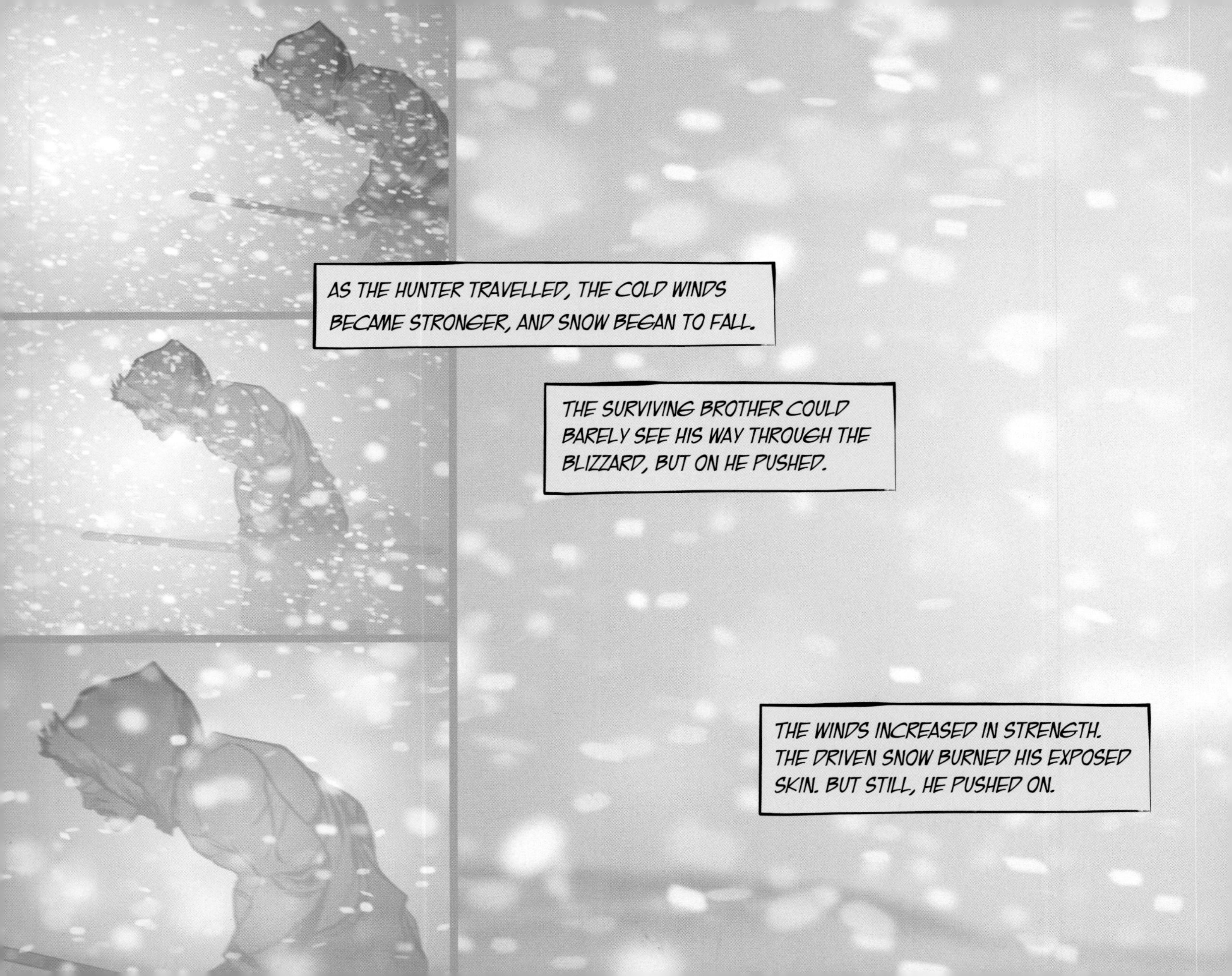
AS THE HUNTER TRAVELLED, THE COLD WINDS BECAME STRONGER, AND SNOW BEGAN TO FALL.
THE SURVIVING BROTHER COULD BARELY SEE HIS WAY THROUGH THE BLIZZARD, BUT ON HE PUSHED.
THE WINDS INCREASED IN STRENGTH. THE DRIVEN SNOW BURNED HIS EXPOSED SKIN. BUT STILL, HE PUSHED ON.

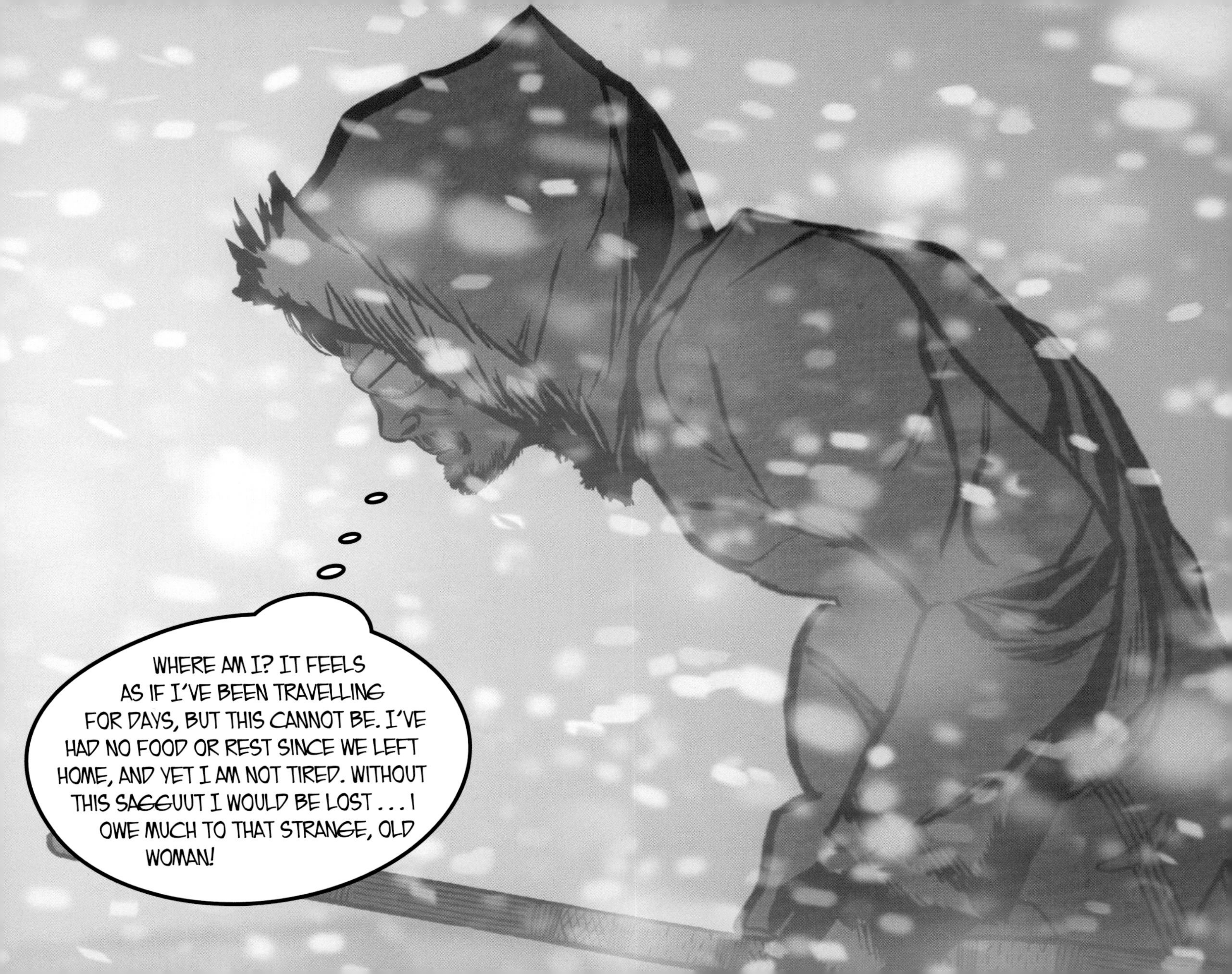
WHERE AM I? IT FEELS AS IF I'VE BEEN TRAVELLING FOR DAYS, BUT THIS CANNOT BE. I'VE HAD NO FOOD OR REST SINCE WE LEFT HOME, AND YET I AM NOT TIRED. WITHOUT THIS SAGGUUT I WOULD BE LOST . . . I OWE MUCH TO THAT STRANGE, OLD WOMAN!

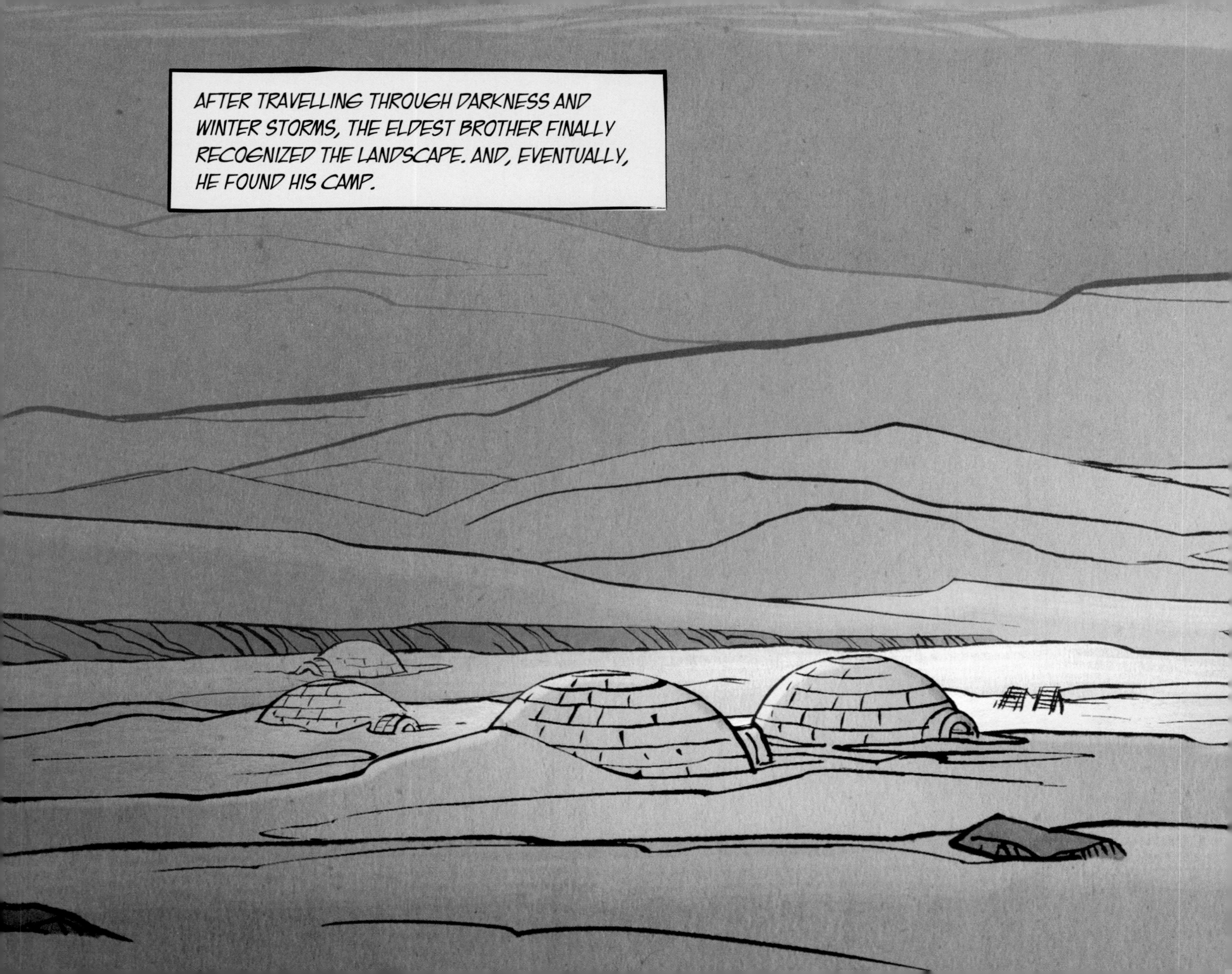
AFTER TRAVELLING THROUGH DARKNESS AND WINTER STORMS, THE ELDEST BROTHER FINALLY RECOGNIZED THE LANDSCAPE. AND, EVENTUALLY, HE FOUND HIS CAMP.

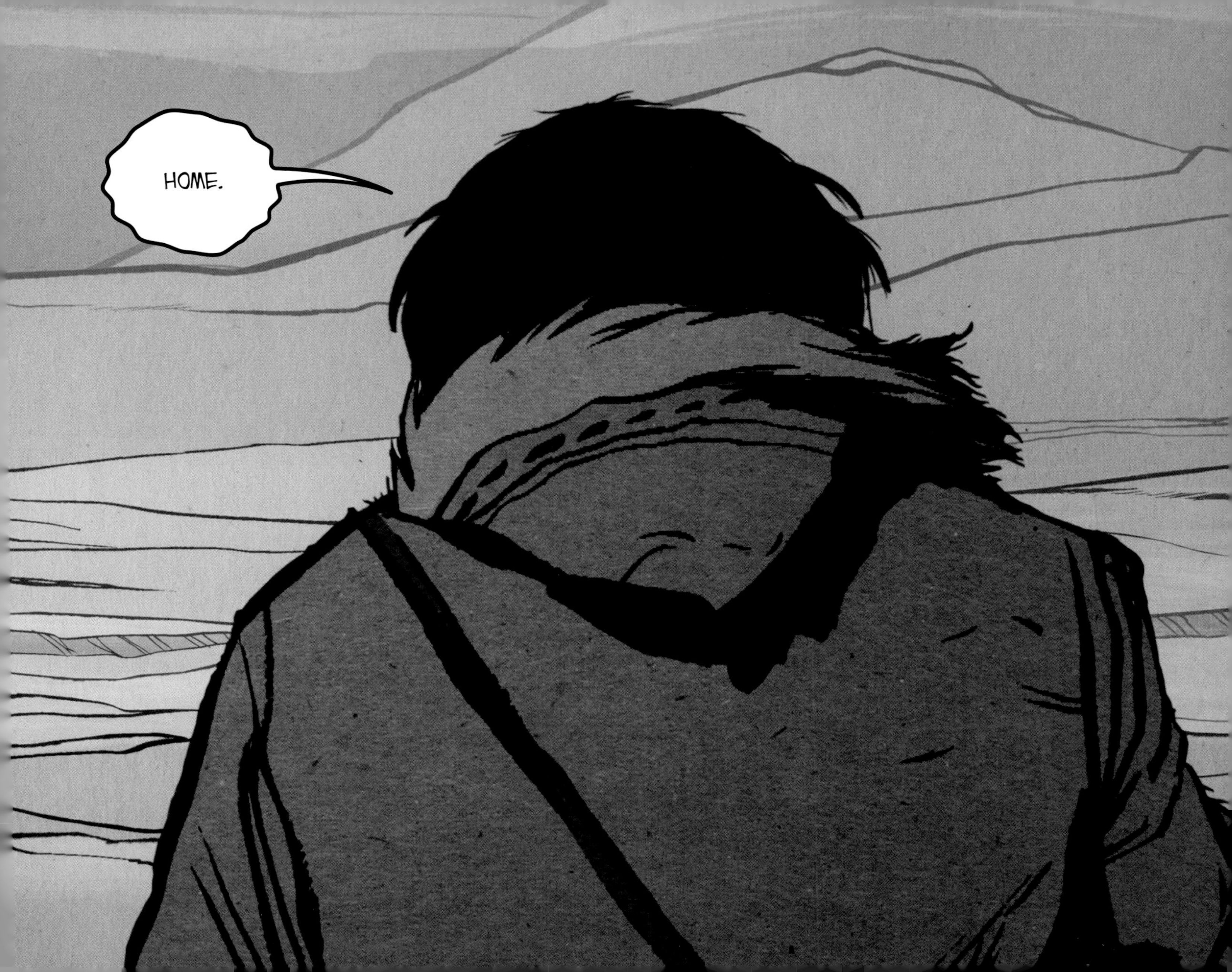
HOME.

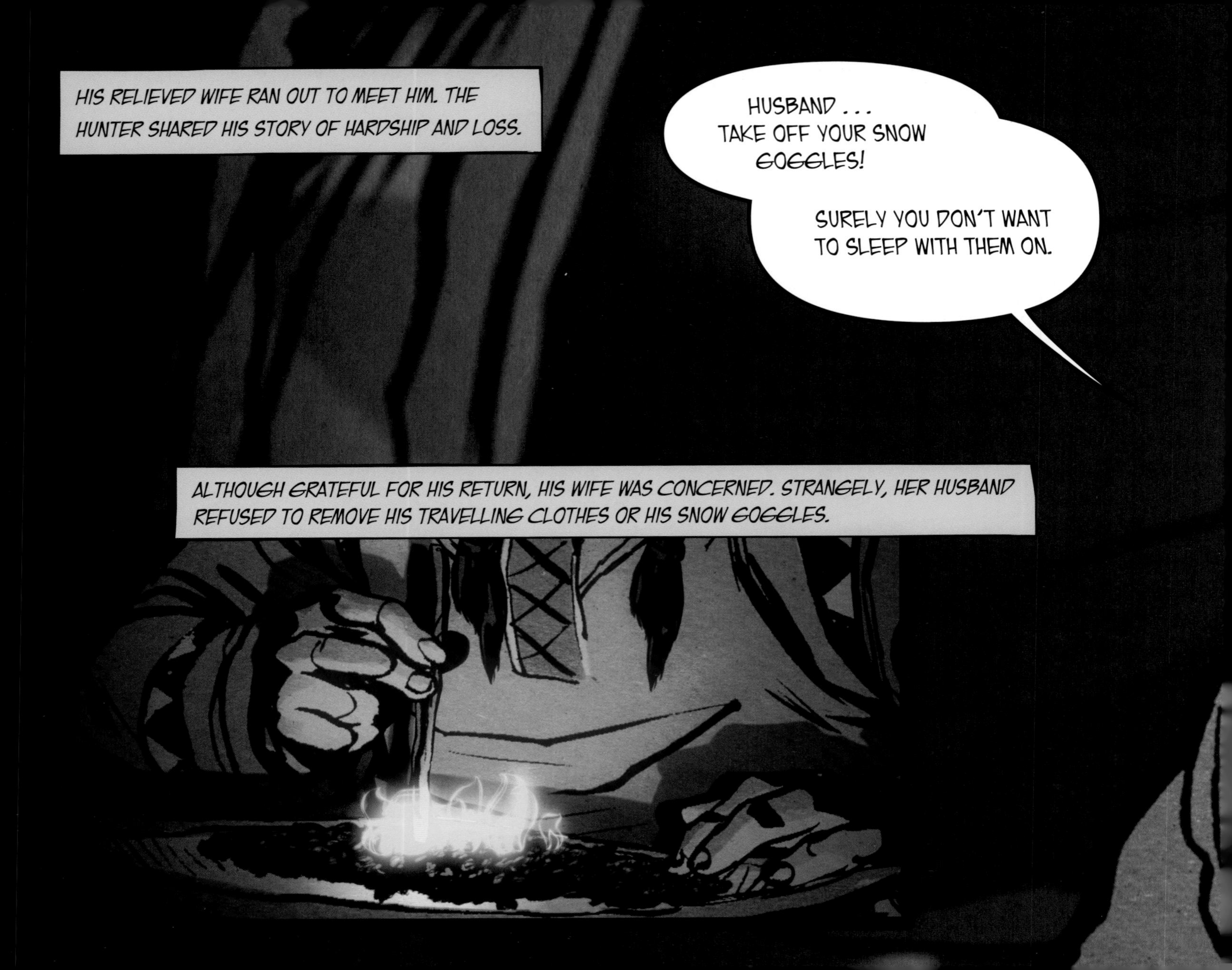
HIS RELIEVED WIFE RAN OUT TO MEET HIM. THE HUNTER SHARED HIS STORY OF HARDSHIP AND LOSS.
HUSBAND . . . TAKE OFF YOUR SNOW GOGGLES!
SURELY YOU DON'T WANT TO SLEEP WITH THEM ON.
ALTHOUGH GRATEFUL FOR HIS RETURN, HIS WIFE WAS CONCERNED. STRANGELY, HER HUSBAND REFUSED TO REMOVE HIS TRAVELLING CLOTHES OR HIS SNOW GOGGLES.

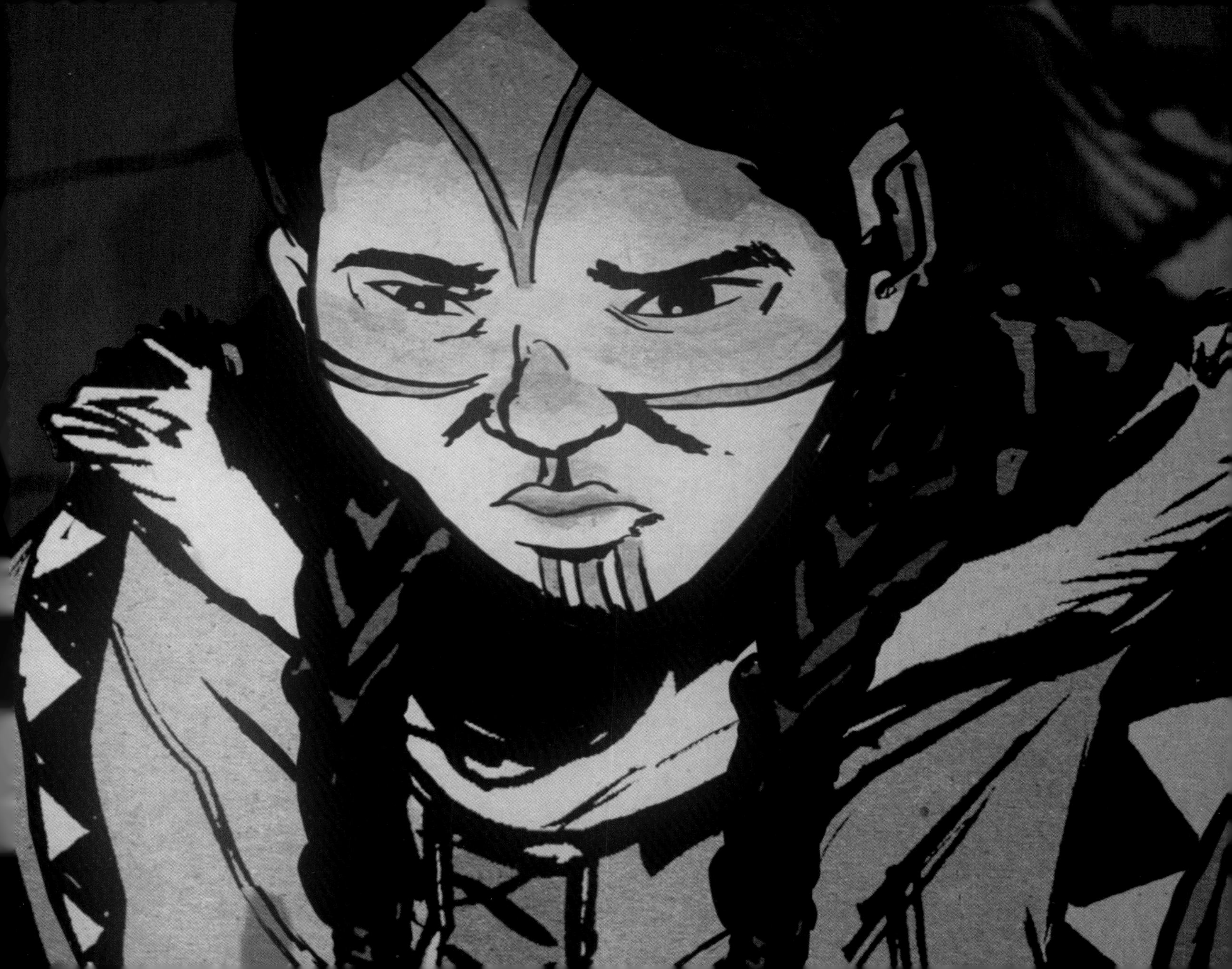

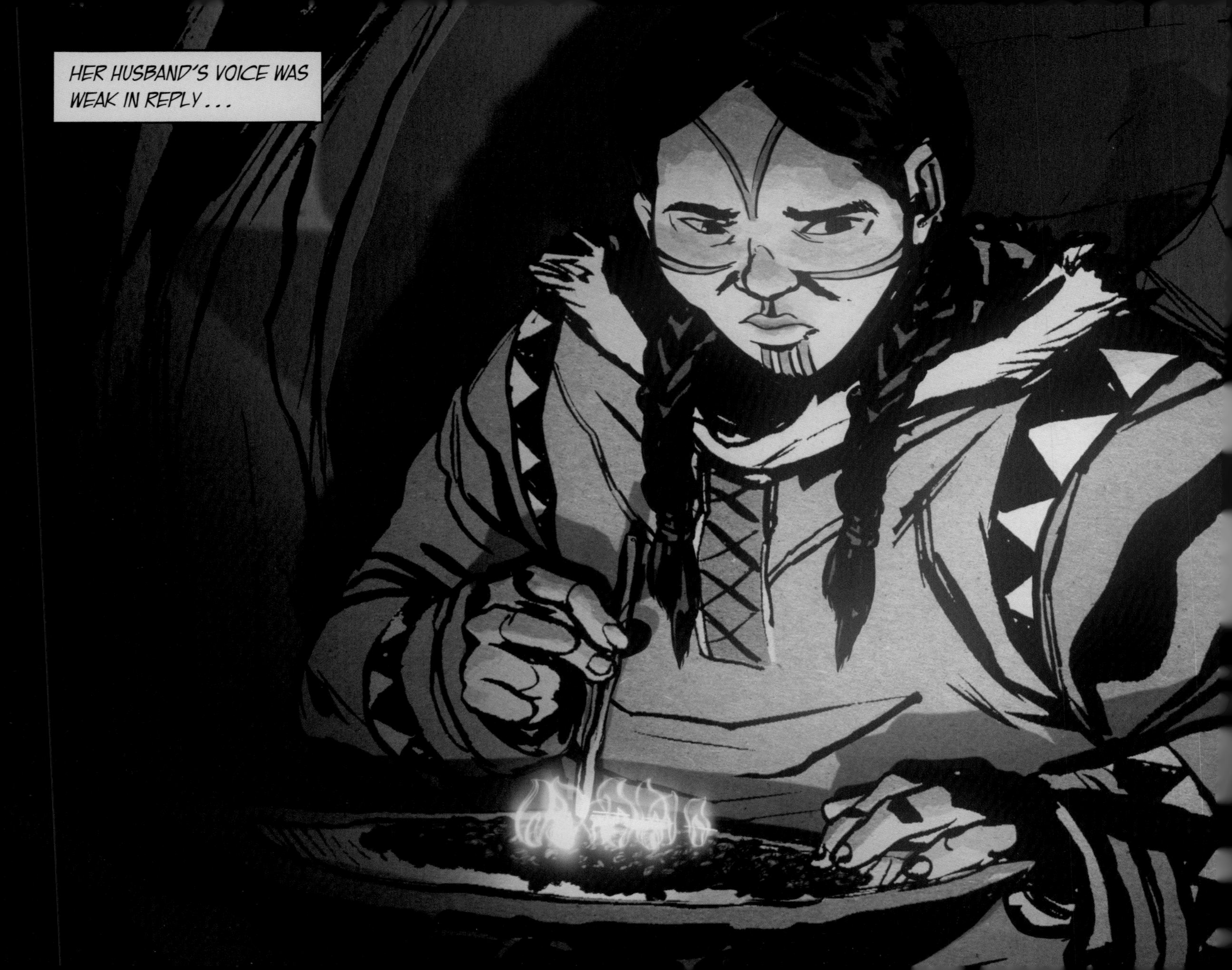
HER HUSBAND'S VOICE WAS WEAK IN REPLY . . .

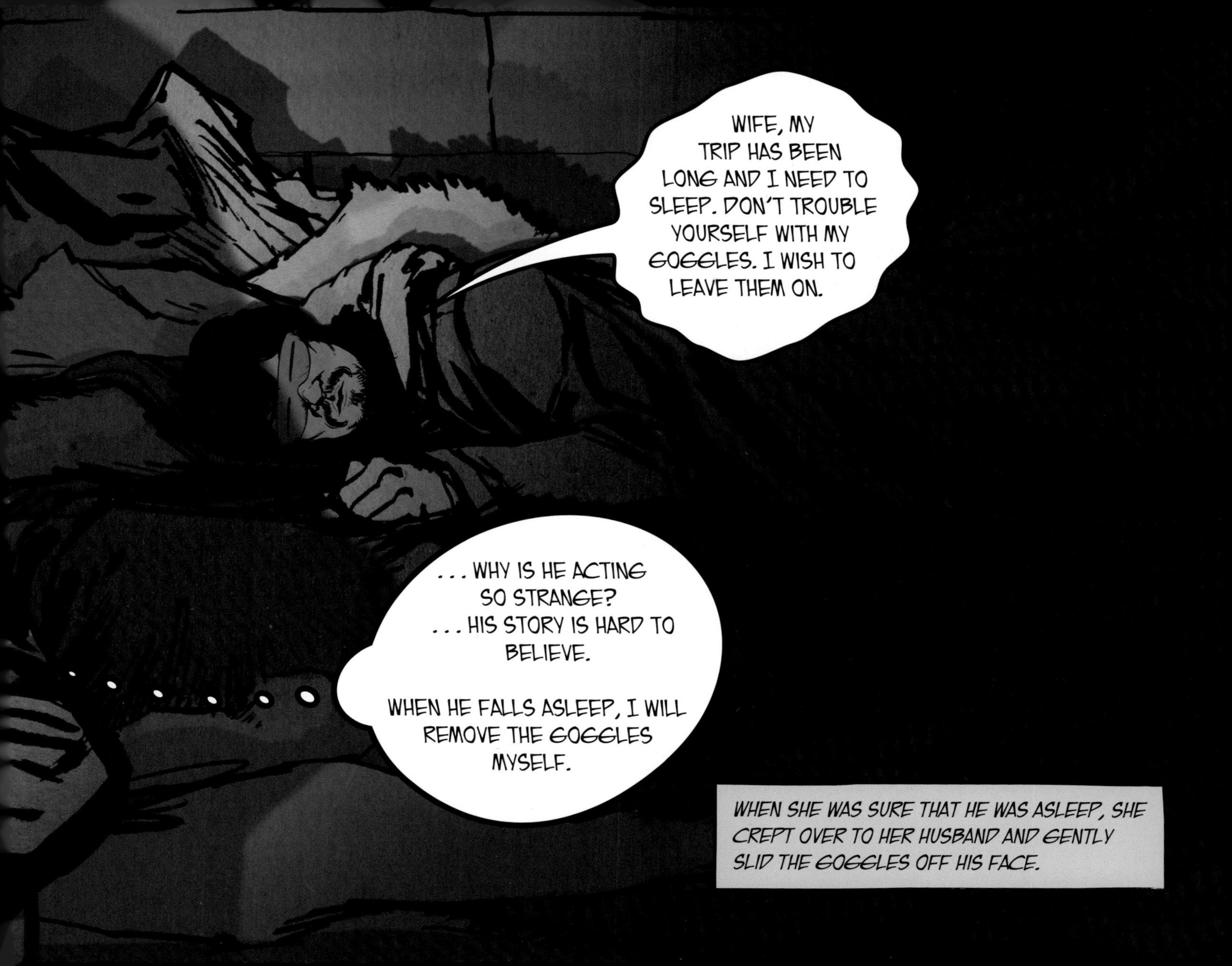
WIFE, MY TRIP HAS BEEN LONG AND I NEED TO SLEEP. DON'T TROUBLE YOURSELF WITH MY GOGGLES. I WISH TO LEAVE THEM ON.
. . . WHY IS HE ACTING SO STRANGE? . . . HIS STORY IS HARD TO BELIEVE. WHEN HE FALLS ASLEEP, I WILL REMOVE THE GOGGLES MYSELF.
WHEN SHE WAS SURE THAT HE WAS ASLEEP, SHE CREPT OVER TO HER HUSBAND AND GENTLY SLID THE GOGGLES OFF HIS FACE.

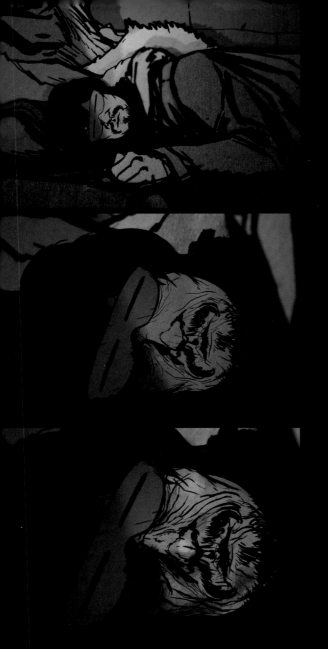

TO HER HORROR, SHE SAW THAT WHERE HIS EYES SHOULD HAVE BEEN, THERE WERE ONLY EMPTY SOCKETS.

AS SHE LOOKED CLOSER, SHE COULD SEE LITTLE SHRIMP LIVING INSIDE HIS SKULL, FEEDING ON HER HUSBAND.

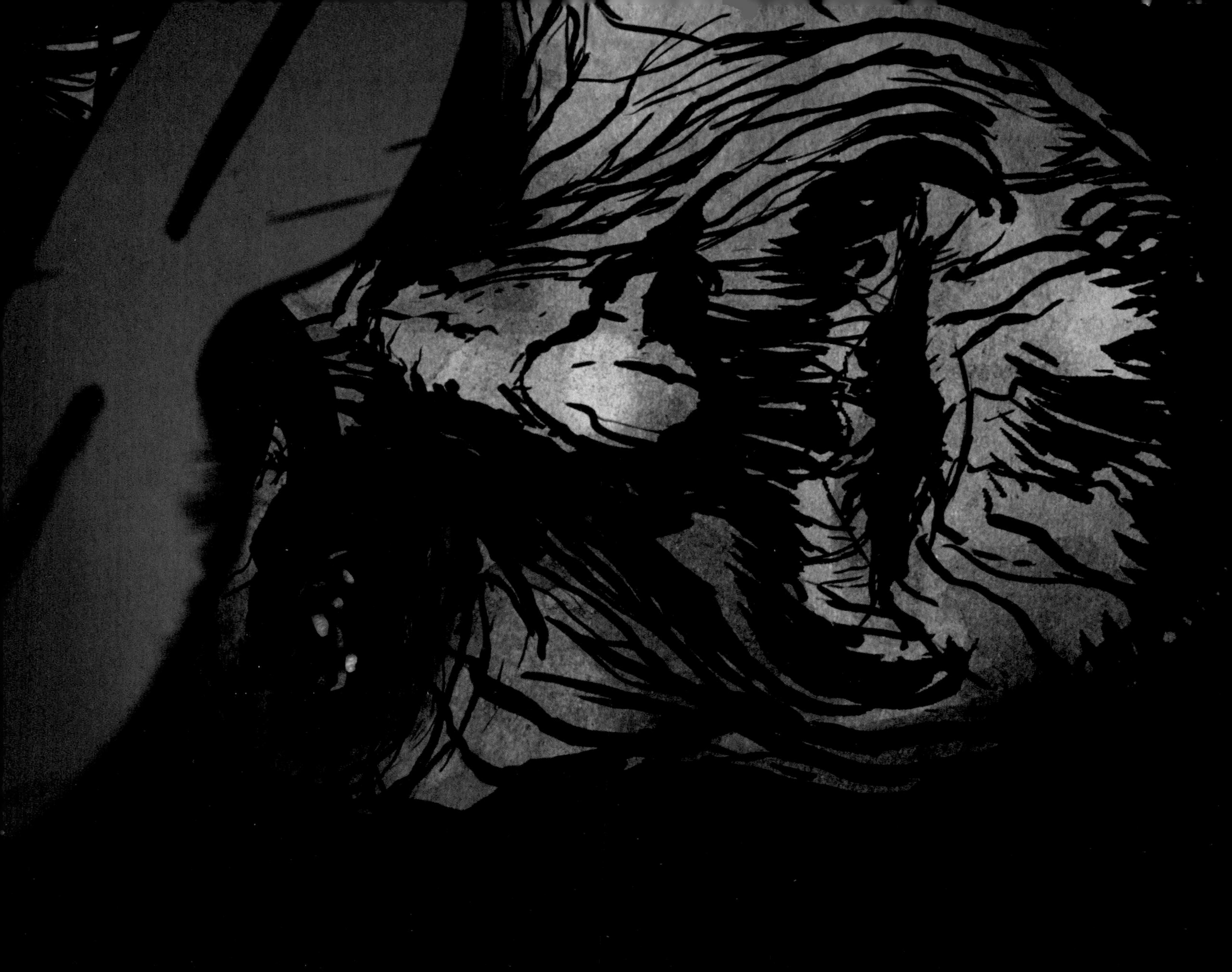

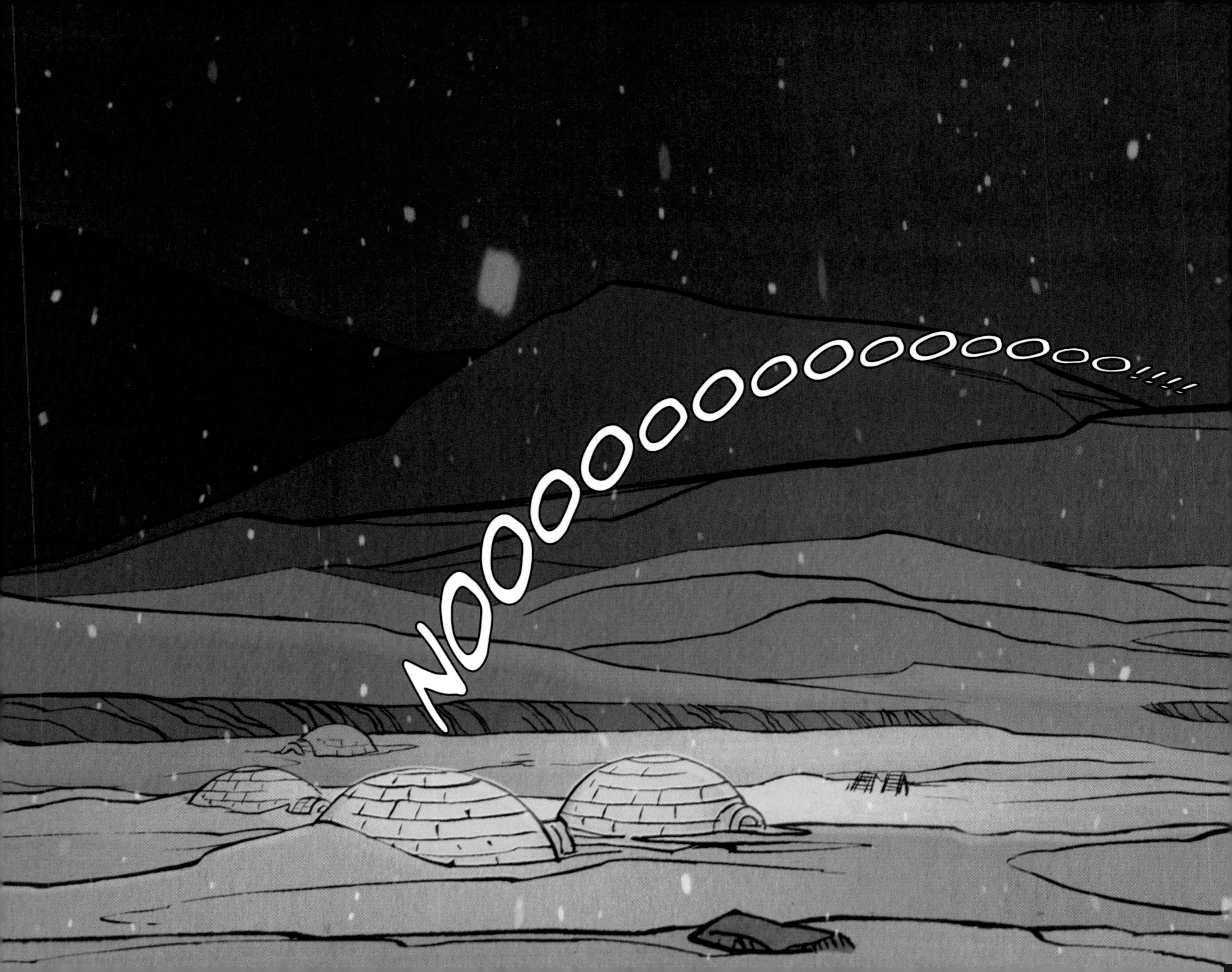
NOOOOOOOOOOOOOO!!!!!

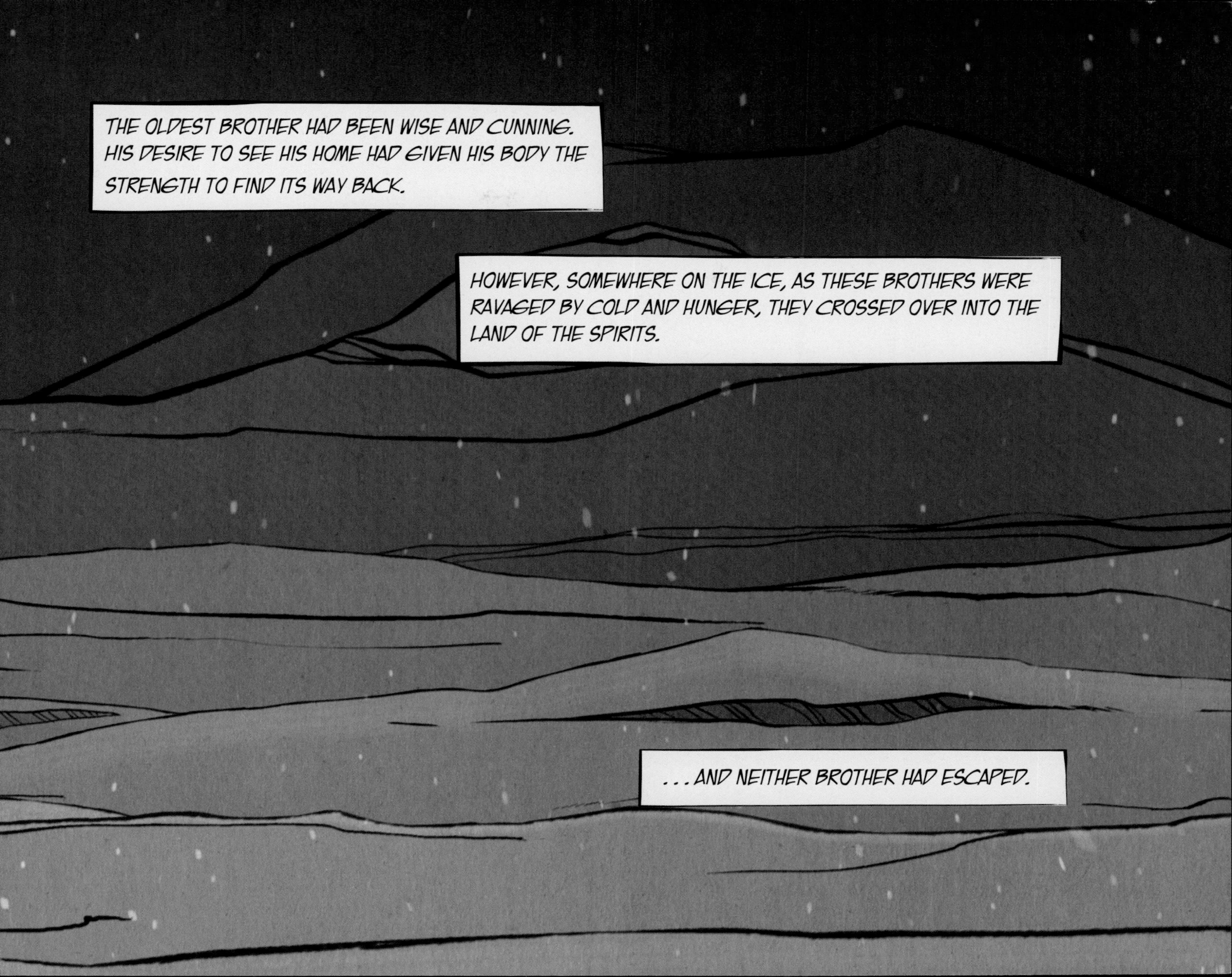
THE OLDEST BROTHER HAD BEEN WISE AND CUNNING. HIS DESIRE TO SEE HIS HOME HAD GIVEN HIS BODY THE STRENGTH TO FIND ITS WAY BACK.
HOWEVER, SOMEWHERE ON THE ICE, AS THESE BROTHERS WERE RAVAGED BY COLD AND HUNGER, THEY CROSSED OVER INTO THE LAND OF THE SPIRITS.
. . . AND NEITHER BROTHER HAD ESCAPED.

THIS BOOK IS DEDICATED TO

MARK KALLUAK

1942 – 2011

MARK'S WISDOM, GENEROSITY, AND KINDNESS WILL REMAIN AN INSPIRATION TO ALL WHO KNEW HIM.

STORY BACKGROUND

"FOR US, STORIES ARE SACRED. THESE TALES LINK US TO OUR ANCESTORS AND TO THE LAND. THEY TELL US OF MAGICAL EVENTS THAT HAPPENED IN THE PAST, BEFORE THE WORLD WAS AS IT IS NOW."

THE COUNTRY OF WOLVES IS ONE OF THESE OLD STORIES. VERSIONS OF THIS FOLKTALE HAVE BEEN PASSED ON FOR GENERATIONS IN COMMUNITIES ACROSS THE ARCTIC. FOR THOSE WHO KNOW INUIT TRADITIONAL BELIEFS, YOU WILL NOTICE SEVERAL REFERENCES TO THE SPIRIT WORLD IN THIS STORY, SUCH AS THE NORTHERN LIGHTS AND THE WATCHFUL MOON. THE FORMER IS A BRIDGE THE DEAD USE TO CROSS OVER INTO THE LAND OF THE SPIRITS, AND THE LATTER IS A PLACE VISITED ON A SPIRIT'S JOURNEY, WHICH IS INHABITED BY BEINGS BOTH KIND AND DANGEROUS. IF YOU LIKED THIS STORY, WE ENCOURAGE YOU TO EXPLORE OTHER INUIT FOLKTALES, AS THE BELIEFS AND HISTORY OF INUIT ANCESTORS ARE ENCODED WITHIN.

LOUISE FLAHERTY AND NEIL CHRISTOPHER
IQALUIT, NUNAVUT, 2012

STORY CONTRIBUTORS

NEIL CHRISTOPHER MOVED TO THE ARCTIC MANY YEARS AGO TO WORK AS AN EDUCATOR. HE HAS WORKED AND LIVED IN MANY OF THE COMMUNITIES IN NUNAVUT. FOR THE LAST DECADE, NEIL HAS BEEN RESEARCHING INUIT MYTHS AND LEGENDS AND HAS USED THIS RESEARCH TO DEVELOP PUBLICATIONS FOR CHILDREN, YOUTH, AND ADULTS. CURRENTLY, NEIL WORKS AS EDITOR FOR INHABIT MEDIA INC.

LOUISE FLAHERTY GREW UP IN CLYDE RIVER, NUNAVUT. EARLY ON, LOUISE WAS FORTUNATE TO BE SURROUNDED BY GREAT STORYTELLERS. HER GRANDPARENTS INSTILLED IN HER A PASSION FOR INUKTITUT, AND AN UNDERSTANDING THAT SPEAKING INUKTITUT IS A FUNDAMENTAL PART OF INUIT IDENTITY. IN 2005, LOUISE CO-FOUNDED INHABIT MEDIA INC., AN INDEPENDENT PUBLISHING HOUSE DEDICATED TO THE PRESERVATION AND PROMOTION OF INUIT KNOWLEDGE AND VALUES AND THE INUKTITUT LANGUAGE. INHABIT MEDIA HAS SINCE PUBLISHED DOZENS OF BOOKS AND INUKTITUT RESOURCES THAT ARE USED IN CLASSROOMS THROUGHOUT NUNAVUT.

DANIEL GIES GREW UP IN ALBERTA, IN THE FOOTHILLS OF THE KANANASKIS VALLEY AT THE FOOT OF THE ROCKY MOUNTAINS. HE STARTED ANIMATING WHEN HE WAS VERY YOUNG, BEGINNING WITH SIMPLE FLIPBOOKS. IT WASN'T LONG BEFORE HIS DAD HAD HIM IN FRONT OF A COMPUTER USING AUTODESK ANIMATOR TO REALIZE HIS CREATIONS, AND HE HASN'T STOPPED SINCE. DANIEL LIVES IN MONTREAL, QUEBEC.

RAMÓN PÉREZ IS A CANADIAN FREELANCE CARTOONIST AND WRITER WORKING PREDOMINANTLY IN COMIC BOOKS, CHILDREN'S BOOKS, AND MAGAZINES AS A GRAPHIC STORYTELLER. RECENT CAREER HIGHLIGHTS INCLUDE *CAPTAIN AMERICA AND THE FIRST THIRTEEN, DEADPOOL TEAM-UP #883*, AND THE EISNER AWARD–WINNING GRAPHIC NOVEL *TALE OF SAND*, WHICH RAMÓN DIRECTLY ADAPTED FROM THE ORIGINAL SCREENPLAY BY JIM HENSON AND JERRY JUHL FOR ARCHAIA PUBLISHING. RAMÓN LIVES IN TORONTO.

INHABIT MEDIA INC.

INHABIT MEDIA INC. IS AN INUIT-OWNED PUBLISHING COMPANY THAT AIMS TO PROMOTE AND PRESERVE THE STORIES, KNOWLEDGE, AND TALENT OF NORTHERN CANADA.

OUR AUTHORS, STORYTELLERS, AND ARTISTS BRING THE NORTH AND TRADITIONAL CULTURE TO LIFE IN A WAY THAT IS ACCESSIBLE TO READERS ACROSS THE WORLD.

AS THE FIRST INDEPENDENT PUBLISHING COMPANY IN NUNAVUT, WE HOPE TO BRING NORTHERN STORIES AND INUIT WISDOM TO THE WORLD.

IF YOU ARE INTERESTED IN LEARNING MORE ABOUT OUR COMPANY, AUTHORS, OR PUBLICATIONS, PLEASE VISIT WWW.INHABITMEDIA.COM.

INHABIT
MEDIA

AMAQQUT NUNAAT:
THE COUNTRY OF WOLVES
– ANIMATED FILM –

THIS GRAPHIC NOVEL IS BASED ON AN ANIMATED FILM ADAPTATION OF THIS TRADITIONAL INUIT STORY.

AMAQQUT NUNAAT: THE COUNTRY OF WOLVES WAS RELEASED IN 2011 AND HAS BEEN AN OFFICIAL SELECTION AT FILM FESTIVALS AROUND THE WORLD SINCE ITS DEBUT. IT HAS ALSO WON SEVERAL INTERNATIONAL AWARDS AND GARNERED CRITICAL ACCLAIM.